KNIT ONE MURDER TWO

A Knitorious Murder Mystery

REAGAN DAVIS

COPYRIGHT

Sign up for Reagan Davis' email list to be notified of new releases: https://www.reagandavis.com/email

ISBN: 978-1-9990435-3-7 (ebook)

ISBN: 978-1-9990435-2-0 (print)

ISBN: 978-1-990228-17-9 (large print paperback)

ISBN: 978-1-990228-01-8 (hardcover)

CONTENTS

CHAPTER 1

TUESDAY SEPTEMBER 10TH

In theory, making half a bed should take half the time as an entire bed. It doesn't. At least not for me. I take just as long to make half the bed as the entire bed. My bed-making skills are an example of Parkinson's Law: "Work expands to fill the time available for its completion."

See also: the junk in my junk drawer expands to fill the entire drawer, my yarn stash expands to fill all the storage in my house, and my wardrobe expands to fill the entire closet when my husband and his wardrobe move out of our bedroom and into the guest bedroom across the hall.

I pull on my favourite jeans and my plum-coloured top, then open the washroom window to clear the steam still lingering from my shower. A generous application of tinted moisturizer, with SPF 30 of course, a touch of mascara around my hazel eyes, and a smear of lip balm complete my makeup routine. With a sigh, I contemplate my damp brown hair. Because curls are unpredictable, it's too soon to tell if today is a good-curl day or a bad-curl day. I slip a hair elastic on my wrist, just in case. Phone in hand, I leave my bedroom with coffee on my mind.

Walking past Adam's room, his unmade bed catches my eye. I close the door so I don't have to see it.

"Just a few more weeks, Megan," I mutter to myself. "Just hang in there a little longer."

With Hannah away at university, Adam can focus on finding an apartment. With any luck, he'll find a place for the first of the month.

Like a woman on a mission, I walk straight to the coffee maker, pop a pod of caramel coffee in the machine and place my *I'd rather be knitting* mug under the spout.

While I wait for it to brew, I open my planner to today's date. I have a 10 a.m. fundraising committee meeting at the Animal Centre, and work from 1 p.m. to 5 p.m. I've been working part time at Knitorious, Harmony Lake's only knitting store and my second home, for just over five years.

I glance at the clock on the microwave. 8:30 a.m.

I have an hour to savour my coffee and some knitting before it's time to leave.

I settle in my favourite corner of the family-room sofa, legs crossed and feet tucked under my butt like a kid in kindergarten who's waiting for story time. I place my phone on the armrest.

"Oscar, play my playlist," I announce to the empty room.

"OK," Oscar replies.

A few seconds later, thanks to the miracle of modern technology, Gwen Stefani's voice fills the quiet space.

Oscar is a digital voice assistant. Hannah and Adam gave him to me for Mother's Day. They love technology, so most holidays I can look forward to getting their new favourite gadget. They make me look more tech-savvy than I am.

Like most technology, Oscar is useful. He can play music, keep my grocery list, provide weather updates, read news headlines, remind me to flip the laundry, and a myriad of other internet-based tasks I haven't tried yet. He is the size of a hockey puck and sits on the end table next to my yarn bowl, where he waits in silence for his next instruction. It's like having a useful pet that never needs food or water.

I savour my much-awaited first sip of coffee and follow the warmth as it travels down my throat and spreads through the rest of my body. I return the mug to the end table and take my knitting out of the yarn bowl.

Ding!

The vibration of my phone makes the sofa shake. It's a text message from a number I don't recognize.

Mystery texter: Hi Mrs. Martel. My name is Fred Murphy. My wife, Stephanie, works with Adam and they've been having an affair.

I didn't see this coming. How did he get my number?

He sends a second message. A screenshot of an intimate text conversation, allegedly between Adam and Stephanie. I know it's easy to fake a text conversation, but I trust the queasiness in my gut. This screenshot is the real deal.

Our marriage has been over for months and Adam is hardly home, even by workaholic lawyer standards. Since Hannah left for university, some nights I'm not sure he comes home at all.

A third text:

Fred: Can we meet to discuss? I have more proof, but I'd like to discuss it with you in person. I can come to Harmony Lake. Let me know when and where.

I immediately text my best friend, April.

Me: Adam's having an affair!

I send a follow-up text, the screenshot of the steamy text exchange.

Me: Her husband wants to meet me. Says he has more to tell me.

April: Wow! Do you want to meet him?

That's a good question. I'm not sure. Fred's texts have piqued my curiosity, that's for sure, and there must be a reason he's reaching out to me. Every instinct I have screams at me to do it.

April: Somewhere public. Meet him at the bakery so T and I can keep an eye on him.

T is what we call April's wife, Tamara. April and Tamara own Artsy Tartsy, the bakery up the street from Knitorious. Tamara is a talented pastry chef, and I stop by to taste her creations every chance I get.

Resolved to find out what Fred wants, I reply to his request for a meeting.

Me: Noon at Artsy Tartsy?

Fred: See you then.

I return my phone to the armrest and pick up my knitting. I'm working on a sock in plain stockinette stitch, a perfect project for knitting in front of the TV or trying to process your feelings about your soon-to-be-ex-husband having a girlfriend. A married girlfriend.

I find my rhythm and work one stitch after another by instinct while my mind replays the text conversation with Fred Murphy.

What is the appropriate reaction to finding out your soon-to-be-ex-husband is seeing someone? I'm not angry. I don't feel betrayed. I'm shocked. It hadn't occurred to me that Adam might have a girlfriend, much less one who's married.

Ding! Dong!

Twenty rounds of knitting and contemplation later, the doorbell brings me back to the here and now. It's April. I know it's her before I put down my knitting. I know because I would do the same thing; I'd rush to her side and make sure she's OK.

April and I have been friends for sixteen years. We met at a mummy-and-me group when Adam, Hannah, and I first moved to Harmony Lake. Our daughters are the same age and best friends. The girls just started university together in Toronto. It comforts us knowing the girls have each other so far from home, and April and I have each other as we adjust to their absence.

When I open the door, April and I have a tight hug. When we pull apart, she hands me a small white confectionery box.

"It's a maple carrot cupcake with pecans, topped with maple cream cheese frosting. T is thinking of adding them to the fall menu and she wants your opinion."

"Halfsies?" I ask over my shoulder, already halfway to the kitchen.

"No, thank you! I ate at least a dozen of them while she tweaked the recipe. I've eaten so many, I dreamed I was being chased by maple carrot cupcake-people, and they were pelting me with pecans."

"More for me!" I sit down at the kitchen table and open the box. "She's outdone herself, April. It's almost too pretty to eat. Almost."

I peel the paper liner away from the cupcake, and April sits in the chair across from me.

"How are you doing?" she asks. "Have you heard anything else from Fred?"

My mouth is full, so I shake my head while I chew.

After I swallow, I say, "I knew it would happen, eventually. It's not like I expect him to spend the rest of his life alone because our marriage didn't work out. I'm just shocked he didn't wait until he moved out, you know? And that she's married."

April nods and stares at me, searching for signs of an emotional breakdown. She's a good friend.

April and I are alike in so many ways. We share the same sense of humour, values, and taste in music. But we are physical opposites. I'm short with an hourglass figure. She's tall and lean. I'm a curly-haired brunette with hazel eyes, while she is a straight-haired blonde with blue eyes. I have fair skin, and she has a perpetual, year-round, sun-kissed glow.

"He could've waited until we announced the separation," I complain. "Other than Hannah, the only people who know are you and Connie."

Connie is my boss at Knitorious, but she's more like family than my boss.

April nods, her mouth pressed into a tight smile.

I finish my cupcake and ask April to please tell T to add it to the menu. It's fabulous and needs to be shared with the entire town as soon as possible.

I shrug. "I'm not in love with Adam anymore." It's cathartic to say it out loud, and a wave of honest relief washes over me. "I love him because he's Hannah's dad, and the three of us will always be a family, you know? But our marriage is definitely over."

My lack of intense feelings about Fred's texts confirm this for me once and for all.

Mindlessly, I twirl my wedding ring with my right hand. I'm a fidgeter, and if I'm not knitting, my hands find something else to keep busy. April reaches across the table and takes my hand, stopping me mid fidget.

"OK, Megastar, but can I ask you one question?" April likes to make up punny nicknames that are puns of my actual name. "If you're at peace with your marriage ending, why do you still wear your wedding ring?" She picks up my left hand and shows it to me as proof.

The ring is a thick band of white gold with a row of square and marquis-cut amethysts—my birthstone—in the centre and a row of diamonds above and below it.

"We agreed to wear them until we announce the separation," I explain. "It was part of our plan not to ruin Hannah's senior year of high school." I shrug. "Also, I love this ring. I designed it myself. When we got married, we were too young and poor to afford an engagement ring. We had simple, white-gold wedding bands. Adam always wanted to upgrade my ring. For our tenth anniversary he told me to pick a ring. I designed this one."

I slip the ring from my left hand to my right. A perfect fit, like it was made for that finger.

"Better?" I ask, holding my right hand in front of April's face.

"As long as you're happy." She smiles and stands up. "Are you ready to head to the bakery and meet Fred?"

CHAPTER 2

IT'S A BEAUTIFUL, sunny day, so we walk to Artsy Tartsy. Soon, the weather will change, and I'll miss walking to Water Street without bundling myself into layers of winter outerwear.

Water Street is to Harmony Lake what Main Street is to other small towns. It's our downtown, and where many of the town's businesses and stores are located. Most of the businesses are on the north side. On the south, a park runs parallel to the lakefront.

Weather permitting, I prefer to walk to work because it's only about a ten-minute walk from my house. Harmony Lake is small geographically and in population. Almost anywhere you need to go is within walking distance. The town is nestled snugly between the lake on the south, and the

Harmony Hills mountain range on the north. Nature left no room for expansion, but provided a perfect foundation for a tourism-based economy.

The Harmony Hills mountain range's two popular ski resorts are booked all winter with skiers and snowboarders, and booked again in the summer with city-escapees who flock to the lakefront. Except for a few weeks in the fall and summer, the town is full of tourists.

Autumn is my favourite time of year. The town is so pretty with the leaves turning shades of red and yellow; the storefronts have their fall window displays set up, and arrangements of pumpkins and fall flowers punctuate the town. Our summer tourist season is over, and the winter tourist season hasn't begun, so for a few precious weeks, we locals have the town to ourselves.

We cross Water Street so we can walk through the park. A few boats dot the lake, and the park is full of townsfolk enjoying the postcard-perfect day.

My phone vibrates in my pocket. It's Adam. I don't have the mental bandwidth to deal with him right now. I clear the notification and return the phone to my pocket.

Across the street, I spot Paul Sinclair walking along the sidewalk in front of The Pharmer's Market, our local pharmacy.

"Shoot!" I duck behind April, then leap to her

left side, hoping her height will shield me from view.

"What is it?" She asks, confused by my sudden ducking and weaving around her.

"It's Paul Sinclair," I reply. "There was a fundraising meeting this morning, and with all the kerfuffle, I forgot. I didn't call and let them know I couldn't make it. You know how he is."

I crane my neck to sneak a peek across the street behind April's back, hoping Paul hasn't spotted me. I'd rather deal with him after I deal with Fred.

It's too late. Paul is crossing the street. He saw me, and now he's catching up with me, probably to scold me for my thoughtlessness and lack of respect for the other committee members who *bothered* to attend the meeting. Paul derives an inordinate amount of satisfaction from chastising his fellow townspeople.

Besides being a member of the Town Council, Paul Sinclair is also the president of the Water Street Business Association (known by the locals as the WSBA), the town council representative on the WSBA board, the WSBA representative on the Town Council, and a member of every committee, organization, and community group in town. To say he's involved in the town is an understatement.

Paul is also Harmony Lake's self-appointed, unofficial bylaw officer. He has a remarkable ability to recite any town bylaw by heart and takes it upon himself to enforce personally every one of them. No matter how minor or justified the infraction.

Paul Sinclair is the town bully.

He doesn't seem threatening at first, but if you violate a bylaw, miss a committee meeting, or otherwise displease him, he'll make sure you know it.

Paul is tall with perfect posture and a year-round tan. His unnaturally white teeth are almost always on display thanks to his carefully molded smile. His smile reminds me of the smile fairy tale wolves have before they eat you or blow down your house.

He even maintains his smile when he's in bully mode, which is confusing when you're his target. I've only ever seen him in a suit, and his dark hair is always perfectly coiffed, because his wife, Kelly, is also his hairdresser. She owns Hairway To Heaven, our local hair salon.

"Megan!" He's almost caught up to us now. April and I stop and turn toward his voice.

My phone vibrates again. Adam. Again. I reject the call and drop the phone in my tote bag.

"Hi Paul." I sigh. "Listen, I'm sorry I missed the fundraising meeting at the Animal Centre this morning. There's been a..."

I've drawn a blank. What do you call an unexpected text message from your husband's potential girlfriend's husband?

"...family emergency...and it took over my day. The meeting completely slipped my mind."

You could call it a family emergency.

"Oh no! Is Hannah OK? Is anyone hurt or anything damaged?" He asks, somehow sounding compassionate and concerned while making me feel like an irresponsible git.

His smile stays constant. His carefully cultivated veneer never cracks.

"Yes," I reply, knowing full well this is a set-up. "Everyone is fine. It's not that kind of emergency."

I attempt my own toothy grin and tilt my head as I look up at him.

"Well, that's a relief! If someone was hurt, I could understand you failing to keep your commitment, but surely you could've called to let us know you would be absent. I mean, imagine if we all just stopped being accountable, and just did whatever we want. It would be chaos, and I'm sure you don't want to contribute to chaos, do you, Megan?"

Still smiling. Him, not me.

I shift my weight from one foot to the other and try to muster the mental fortitude to defend myself. I'm laser focused on this meeting with Fred.

"This is the first meeting I've missed, Paul. Ever. I always follow through with my commitments, except for this morning, which was unavoidable. I'm sure you and the other committee members had a productive meeting, despite my absence. Please forward the meeting minutes to me, and I'll look them over before the next meeting." I'm not in the mood for his bullying right now.

"Will you have time to read the minutes with this emergency? Maybe if you told me what the emergency is, I could help."

He's not trying to be helpful; he's being nosy and condescending.

"Actually, Megan, I was hoping to speak with you alone after the meeting about a different matter. Do you have a few minutes now? Or we could meet later, as long as it's today. We can talk about the meeting and discuss the other thing."

"Today isn't good for me, Paul. You can email the minutes to me along with whatever else you want to discuss."

I sneak a peek at Paul's watch. Almost noon. We need to get to Artsy Tartsy.

"Just fifteen minutes later today?" he implores.

He's not letting this go.

"Paul, we're in a hurry." April holds up her right hand between Paul and me with her palm facing Paul in a stop gesture. "Megan told you why she missed the meeting, and she apologized. Let it go. Email the meeting notes to her and if she has questions, she'll call you."

As April finishes speaking, she grabs my hand and starts walking fast toward the bakery, dragging me along like a fed-up mother pulling a determined toddler away from the toy aisle in a store. Her long legs take longer strides than me, so I do an awkward shuffle-walk-jog to catch up with her.

"Thank you," I say, giving April's hand a squeeze.

She reciprocates my squeeze, looks down at me, and winks.

"The only way to deal with bullies is to confront them," she insists. In a softer voice she adds, "You're going to be OK, you know. You and Hannah always have T and I, and whatever happens today with this Fred person, we've got your back."

We're more than friends; we're family.

CHAPTER 3

As soon as we walk into Artsy Tartsy, the intoxicating aroma of fresh-baked pastries and bread envelop me like a hug. I inhale deeply and the comforting smell fills me with warmth.

I smile and wave to Tamara, who is serving a customer behind the long, glass counter. Tamara smiles and waves back. Without turning her head, she raises her eyebrows and moves her eyeballs to the left toward a man sitting alone at one of the bistro tables, staring at his phone.

April wishes me luck under her breath and hovers a few steps behind me as I approach his table.

"Fred?"

I extend my right hand for him to shake. He looks up at me from his phone.

"Megan?"

We shake hands.

"The owners have offered us the use of the office so we can speak in private," I say.

I gesture toward the back of the bakery. Fred stands up and follows me to the office with April in tow.

The office is a small, windowless room with a simple white desk, two chairs, and a low profile, white filing cabinet. The walls, floor, and ceiling are also white, which makes the room feel less small and dark. There are accents of teal on the upholstery and teal office supplies. Family photos in teal frames of April, Tamara, and their two kids dot the walls.

I claim the chair closest to the door. Safety first. Fred has no choice and sits in the other chair.

He's tall and thin, with a wiry physique, light brown hair, a receding hairline, and glasses. I'd guess early thirties. His vibe is casual; jeans, a leather belt with an oversize, metal buckle, running shoes, and a button-down plaid shirt. He wears a plain gold wedding band.

From the doorway, April offers refreshments. Fred declines, and I ask for a glass of water. In part because I'm thirsty, and in part so she'll have a reason to come back. She closes the door behind her when she leaves.

Fred unlocks his phone and reveals more

screenshots of alleged text conversations between his wife, Stephanie, and Adam. I'm about to ask him how I can verify the screenshots are real when he swipes again, showing me an intimate and revealing photo of Adam.

His face isn't in the photo, but there's no doubt it's Adam. A photo like this is harder to fake than a text conversation.

Fred scrolls through more intimate photos of Adam, then offers to text me the proof. Rendered momentarily speechless from shock, I nod. He explains how he discovered the affair two days ago when, by accident, Stephanie sent him a photo of Adam instead of a photo of their cat in a cardboard box.

Fred says when he confronted Stephanie, she confessed and told him everything. She even gave him access to her phone.

How could Adam be so stupid! I can't count how many times we lectured Hannah about the dangers of sending photos to people on the internet. You never know when those photos will come back to haunt you, or who else will see them. Yet here he is, sending compromising photos of himself to some random woman, who shared them with her husband, who then shared them with me. How many other people have seen these? Or, heaven forbid, have copies. Unbelievable.

A gentle knock at the door distracts me from my

inner rant. April has a tray with water and a small plate of pastries to sample. She stands behind Fred so he can't see her.

"Are you OK?" she mouths, exaggerating her words so I can read her lips.

I smile and nod. She asks if we need anything else, then reminds us she's just outside if we do. She leaves and closes the door behind her.

I cross my legs and lean toward Fred.

"What do you want, Fred?" I ask. "We didn't need to meet face-to-face for you to send me your proof. You must want something."

"We want Adam to leave the firm," he replies.

Fred said *we.* His wife knows he's here. They're working together. He waits for me to speak. I stay silent, worry my lips between my teeth, and maintain constant eye contact. Don't show any signs of weakness, Megan.

"Stephanie and I are working it out, but it can't happen if she works with Adam every day," he explains. "Stephanie is a junior associate, and Adam is a senior partner. It would be easier for him to find another job than her."

He takes a deep breath and adds, "Their relationship violates the firm's fraternization policy. Also, as a senior partner, Adam is in a position of authority over Stephanie, and it could appear to the other partners that his influence as her superior coerced her into having an affair with him."

Anger bubbles up from somewhere deep inside me. My mouth is dry and hot, and my face is flushing with heat. I sip my water and try to compose myself.

I'm well aware of the firm's fraternization policy, and so is Adam since he wrote it. It states employees cannot date or engage in intimate, personal relationships with other employees.

Did Adam use his position as partner to coerce her into having an affair? For years he has passionately represented victims of workplace harassment. I've seen how disgusted he is with the perpetrators; the Adam I know would never do this. But I guess that's what the wife always says when stories like this become public.

I pull myself up to my full seated height. "Are you implying my husband *forced* your wife to have an intimate relationship with him?"

I try hard to remain calm and composed, but the hostile, defensive tone in my voice betrays me.

Fred shifts in his chair and averts his eyes to his hands, which he's wringing in his lap.

"No." He shakes his head, still staring at his hands. "Stephanie says she made the first move, and I believe her."

He sits up, composes himself, and adds, "But that doesn't change the fact that the firm has a strict policy prohibiting employees from dating each other. Adam is technically her superior, and the firm has a history of representing victims of workplace harassment. The optics of this relationship wouldn't be good for the firm's reputation, or your husband's."

There it is. Fred and Stephanie Murphy are using the photos and screenshots to blackmail Adam into leaving the firm. Fred is right about one thing. A scandal like this would damage Adam's career, and maybe even end it.

It could ruin us financially when we have university expenses, and a separation that's about to add the costs of a second household to our family budget.

How will we explain this to Hannah?

"You said, 'we want Adam to leave the firm.' Do you mean *we* as in you and Stephanie? She knows you're here today? Are you speaking on behalf of both of you?"

"Yes." He nods. "She knows I'm here. She told me to speak to you in person to avoid a technological trail of evidence."

I clear my throat to stop myself from laughing out loud at the irony. The Murphys don't want any technological evidence, yet they're using a technological smoking gun to blackmail my family. She's a lawyer for crying out loud, an officer of the court, and she's taking part in blackmail.

Fred's expression is dead serious. I don't think the Murphys are bluffing, I believe they'll follow through with their threat if Adam doesn't leave the firm.

"What EXACTLY are you asking ME to do?" My volume increases in proportion to my decreasing patience.

No more proof or explanations. Just tell me what I need to know. I need to get away from Fred Murphy before I throw up.

"We expect today to be Adam's last day at the firm. Steph called in sick yesterday and today, but she's going back to work tomorrow. If Adam is still there, she'll go straight to the partners. I met with Adam earlier, and he knows what we expect. I thought you should know. You're a victim, like me. You and I are collateral damage, victims of this mess. But encourage him to do the right thing, so you and your daughter won't have to deal with the fallout if he doesn't."

"Does Adam know you contacted me?" I ask, wondering if this is why Adam has been blowing up my phone with calls and texts all morning.

"No, he doesn't," Fred shakes his head. "I'll leave that up to you."

"I see." I stand up and squeeze the doorknob, my knuckles white from channelling my pent-up emotions into my grip. "I'd say it was nice to meet you, Fred, but it wasn't." I flash him an insincere smile. "Enjoy the rest of your day."

Fred stands up, and I step into the bakery so he

can walk past me and leave. I pick up the water and a plate of pastries, follow him to the door, and watch him leave. Good riddance.

The bakery is empty. Tamara comes out from behind the counter and locks the door behind Fred. She turns the OPEN sign to CLOSED and wraps her arms around me. Feeling safe now that Fred is gone, I cry.

I tell April and Tamara about my conversation with Fred. Then, compose myself, dry my tears, and thank them for letting me use the office and always having my back.

It's almost time for my shift at Knitorious, and I need to tell Connie everything that's happened.

Tamara accompanies me to the door, and as she unlocks it, she makes a joke about flipping the CLOSED sign to OPEN before Paul Sinclair hears Artsy Tartsy is closed and comes rushing over to recite and enforce the many bylaws that are probably violated when a Water Street business closes in the middle of a business day. We chuckle and I step into the warmth of the midday sun.

It's not even 1 p.m., and today already feels like the longest day of my life.

On the walk to Knitorious, I reach into my bag and retrieve my phone. Adam phoned and texted again when I was with Fred.

I'm trying to work out what to say to Adam, when I notice Paul Sinclair and Fred Murphy.

Together. Sitting in a car in front of a parking meter. Both men are animated and have angry expressions on their faces. They're so engrossed in their discussion, they don't notice me.

As I pass the parked car, I slow my pace to hear them. I can't hear a word, but they're speaking at the same time, and their facial expressions and exaggerated hand gestures make me think they're arguing. The two people who tried to bully me are shouting at each other. I think this is what April would call karma.

What could they be arguing about? Maybe Paul is reprimanding Fred for parking wrong. Or not putting enough money in the meter. Or violating some other bylaw.

I'm so distracted thinking about their heated discussion that I almost walk right past Knitorious.

CHAPTER 4

THE JINGLE of the bell over the door comforts me. Stepping into Knitorious always relaxes and inspires me. It's my second home.

The store is spacious with dark wood floors and yarn-filled, white shelving along the walls. The counter is in the centre. Behind it there is a long wooden harvest-style table with ten chairs where we teach classes and sit at knit night. The cozy sitting area is in front of the counter, off to the side. Knitorious is classic yet contemporary, just like its owner, Connie.

Connie stands at the winding station with her back to me. The winding station is a small wooden table with a yarn swift and ball winder attached to it. A yarn swift is a wooden contraption that holds a skein of yarn while it's being wound into a ball. We wrap the skein of yarn around the yarn swift, then attach one end of the yarn to the ball winder. We crank the ball winder so the swift spins and pulls the yarn from the skein to the ball that's being wound. Aside from knitting itself, winding yarn is the most meditative knitting activity there is.

I walk toward Connie, but stop at the harvest table when Harlow, Connie's cat, flops onto the tabletop and exposes his belly. Unable to resist his soft under fluff, I'm compelled to rub him. He knows I can't resist his fluffiness. His body rumbles with purrs as soon as I touch his soft, warm tummy.

"It's been a heck of a day so far!" I declare.

I'm eager to fill in Connie on the events of this morning, but she turns, raises her left index finger to her closed lips in a shushing gesture, then bends her finger to her right. My gaze follows her finger, landing on Kelly Sinclair, who's browsing in the bulky yarn section. I nod to Connie, acknowledging her message.

I stash my tote bag under the counter and admire the skeins of ice-blue, bulky yarn on the counter.

"This is beautiful," I say, petting and squishing the yarn. "Is it new?"

The yarn tag says it's a bulky weight, merino-cashmere blend, and the colour name is *Breathless*.

"These skeins are going to be a new wrap for my sister." Kelly turns from the shelf of yarn where she's browsing and walks toward me. "She's always complaining her office is freezing. This colour is perfect for her!" She joins me with her perfectly manicured hands in petting and squishing the skeins of yarn. "Isn't it gorgeous?!

Kelly owns Hairway to Heaven. She and Paul live in the apartment above the salon. Kelly is nothing like her husband. She's pleasant, genuine, and kind. The opposite of her pushy bully of a husband.

Kelly is one of the most glamorous women in Harmony Lake. Her long, blonde hair is always blown out, so it's smooth and bouncy, her make-up is applied with professional precision, and her nails are meticulously manicured. She wears classic, elegant clothes, and her smile lights up a room. She's a walking testimonial to the services her salon provides. Sometimes, I wonder what she and Paul have in common. They're living proof that opposites attract.

"Connie offered to wind a skein for me," Kelly explains, "so I can cast on between clients. I doubt I'll get the chance, though, I'm booked for the rest of the day." Kelly checks the time on her phone, then retrieves her wallet from her purse. "And... oh... look at the time! I have to get back. Mrs.

Willows is coming in for roots and highlights at 2 p.m., and the plumber said he'd come by to clear the drain after 1:30 p.m. I should go before I'm distracted by more yarn!" She giggles.

"Is it Archie or Ryan who's coming to unclog the drain?" I ask.

Archie and Ryan Wright are Harmony Lake's local father-son handyperson service. Most of the businesses on Water Street, and pretty much everyone else in town, rely on them for handy work and repair jobs. Their white van with the words "The Wright Men For The Job," painted on the side in red letters, is a common sight around Harmony Lake.

"We don't hire Archie and Ryan anymore." Kelly's smile disappears, and a more serious expression appears in its place. "Paul says Ryan isn't trustworthy. He said Ryan isn't welcome in the salon or the apartment ever again."

"Oh. Did Paul say why?"

I've heard no one complain about either Archie or Ryan. Ever.

Kelly shakes her head. "No, Paul just said he doesn't trust him and doesn't want me to hire him." She shrugs and pulls her credit card from her wallet.

Connie stops winding and grabs a pair of large knitting needles from the needle display. The fifteen-millimetre wooden needles look more like drum sticks than knitting needles. Bulky yarn requires big needles.

"If you don't get gauge with these, Kelly, just bring them back, and we'll exchange them for a different size." Connie smiles.

Connie hands me the needles, and I ring them up. Kelly pays, I put her yarn and needles in a paper bag with handles, and she rushes out the door to beat Mrs. Willows and the plumber to Hairway to Heaven.

"What do you think that's about? Paul not trusting Ryan?" I ask Connie now that we're alone.

Connie waves her hand in front of her face like she's waving away an unpleasant smell. "Who knows? Paul is always picking on someone, and if he's not picking on them today, he's looking for a reason to pick on them tomorrow. You know how he is, I'm sure it's something from nothing."

I reach under the counter and retrieve my knitting bag from my tote bag. I've carried around this purple yarn for a week, waiting for the chance to cast on a new hat and cowl for Hannah.

I take my knitting to a sofa and settle in. While I knit, I tell Connie about the texts from Fred, the encounter April and I had with Paul Sinclair, my meeting with Fred, the blackmail scheme, and the weird argument I saw between Fred and Paul on my way here. I'm trying to knit while I talk, but

Harlow decides he'd rather nap on my lap than on the table, so I put my knitting aside to stroke the purring, sleepy cat.

Connie is a superb listener and a source of sage advice. I know she worries about Hannah and me, especially with the separation. I don't want her to worry more than she already does, but not telling her would feel like lying. I tell her and April almost everything. She even introduces me to people as her daughter-friend, and I call her my mother-friend.

At sixty-eight years young, Connie is the smartest, most sophisticated woman I know. She's wise in the ways of the world, yet the concept of sexting seems to elude her. She keeps asking how I can be certain it's Adam in the photos if his face isn't in any of them.

Without being explicit, I assure Connie it's definitely him in the photos. She's worried the photos are fake, and we're being conned. She asks to see them for herself. Obviously, that can't happen, so to stop this awkward conversation from becoming even more awkward, I tell her Adam's tattoo is in the photos. Adam has Hannah's birth date tattooed in roman numerals over his heart.

Thankfully, she accepts this and stops asking to see them. I change the subject, and we discuss ideas for the fall window display.

I'm pretty sure this isn't a lie because I recall

seeing his tattoo in at least one photo, but I'm not certain. I haven't looked at them since Fred sent them to me. I'd like very much never to see them again.

When Connie gets up to answer the landline, I check my phone and find more calls and texts from Adam.

How do I tell him I know about the affair? At a loss for words, I send him a screenshot of the text conversation between him and Stephanie, careful to send him the least intimate one. As soon as I hit send, three dots on the screen indicating Adam is typing a reply.

Adam: I'm sorry. I will take care of this today. You spoke to Paul?

What does *taken care of* mean? Does that mean he's leaving the firm, or does it mean something else? He knows Paul was looking for me? I miss one meeting in sixteen years and Paul calls my husband? Seems like a bit of an overreaction on Paul's part, but OK.

Me: Yes, he found me on my way into town.

I want to tell him about my meeting with Fred, but I'm a bit paranoid about putting it in a text since I've got a phone full of incriminating photos and screenshots of text conversations that are being used against my family. I hit send and no dots appear. Instead, my phone rings with Adam's name appearing on the screen.

"Hi," I whisper, aware Connie is on the phone in the kitchenette behind the store.

I stretch to look through the doorway. Her back is to me, her sleek, shoulder-length silver hair bobbing as she talks on the phone.

Connie is an animated talker. She uses her hands and facial expressions to add emphasis when she speaks. If people were books, most of us would be novels, but Connie would have full colour illustrations. She uses gestures to add context to what she's saying.

"Meg, I'm so sorry. I didn't know this would happen."

"Which part didn't you know, Adam?" I hiss. "That your girlfriend is married? That dating an employee is against the company policy *you* wrote? That you're technically her boss? That they could use those photos against us? That sleeping with an employee might hurt your career? That I might see a bunch of photos I wish I didn't know exist? You'll need to be more specific, Adam."

There's a long, angry silence. Well, angry on my end; for Adam, it might be an awkward silence.

"I know I messed up, Meg, and I'm fixing it. I've been in meetings with the other partners all day, and I'll be here late tonight tying up loose ends. If you're still awake when I get home, I'd like to talk, and explain things to you. If it's too late tonight, maybe we can talk tomorrow."

He says he'll be late like it's a rare occurrence, like he hasn't been working late and bringing work home with him on weekends for the better part of fifteen years. We need to talk about this, though, he's right.

"Fine," I agree, sighing. "Let's talk tonight or tomorrow."

I'm about to ask him what "taking care of it" means, but I'm interrupted by the jingle of the bell over the door. A local yarn dyer is struggling to hold the door open while carrying a tub of yarn that Connie must have ordered. I tell Adam I have to go. We end the call, and I rush to hold the door for the dyer.

In between serving customers, helping a knitter recover a stitch she dropped about three hundred rows ago, and petting Harlow on demand, I unpack the tub of yarn, add the skeins to the store inventory, take photos of them for the shopping section of the store website, and rearrange some shelves to make room for the new, fall-coloured skeins.

Harlow and I look at each other when we hear dishes clinking. Harlow's pupils dilate, his tail twitches, and his ears are at attention. He's on full alert. The *ffffffffpp* of a lid peeling off a can of cat food confirms his suspicion that it's dinner time. He runs to the back of the store and into the kitchenette. He meows loudly when the spoon *tinks* against his dish as Connie doles out the gross-smelling loaf of cat food.

How is it dinner time already? According to the clock on the cash register, it's 6:20 p.m. We should have closed twenty minutes ago. I get up to lock the door and turn the sign to CLOSED. When I get there, it's already locked, and the sign turned.

"I closed up twenty minutes ago, my dear." Connie is out of the kitchenette and sitting at the harvest table. "You were so focused that you didn't notice."

"I was focused on keeping busy. To keep my mind off Murphygate." It didn't work.

Credit goes to April for coming up with, Murphygate. She used it a couple of hours ago when she texted me for an update.

"Have you heard anything from Adam or the Murphygate people, my dear?"

Connie's reference to the *Murphygate people* makes me smile.

"I would tell you if I did. I'm hoping no news is good news, and I'll never hear from them again."

"You should stay for supper tonight. We'll make tacos and drink wine. We can watch that British murder mystery show we like and have a sleepover! We haven't had a girls' night in ages." Connie claps her hands in front of her, like she just thought up the best idea ever.

Connie dotes on me. She's choosing tonight for

a girls' night to help keep my mind off Murphygate, and to stay close in case there's another dramatic development.

"I'd love a girls' night, but can we do it another time? Today was exhausting and I think I'd fall asleep in my tacos and wine."

I'm moving around the store, picking up mislaid skeins of yarn, and returning them to their proper shelves when the half-wound skein of "Breathless" yarn at the winding station catches my eye.

"Kelly was in a rush and left without it," I say, nodding toward the winding station.

"Oh mothballs! I completely forgot to finish winding it." Connie turns around in her chair and starts cranking the ball winder.

I finish tidying the store while Connie finishes winding the skein of yarn.

"I'll drop it off on my way home," I offer. "I have to walk past the salon, anyway."

I place the yarn in a small bag and drop it in my tote. Connie follows me to the door so she can lock it behind me.

"I'll see you in the morning." I open my arms for a hug.

Connie squeezes me and rubs my back.

"Call me tonight if you need anything." She pulls away and points at my nose. "I mean it. I don't care how late it is."

"I will, I promise! Goodnight."

The lock clicks behind me as I walk down the street.

CHAPTER 5

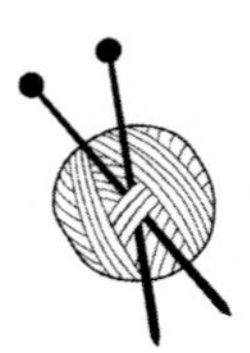

IT'S AFTER HOURS, but the lights are on inside the salon, so I check the salon door before heading around to the back door that leads to the upstairs apartment.

I grip the handle and read the business hours posted on the door. The salon closes at 6 p.m. on Tuesdays. It's almost 7 p.m. now. I pull, but the door is locked. I try pushing it anyway, because I've made that mistake before, and determine it's definitely locked.

Bringing my right hand to my forehead to reduce the glare of the setting sun reflecting off the salon window, I squint.

Kelly is standing at a sink tending to a client. Her back is to me. I pull the yarn from my tote bag and knock on the window. When Kelly turns around, I wave, smile, and hold up the bag. She smiles in acknowledgement, turns to her client, then turns back to me and walks toward the door, wiping her hands on a black towel with a pink, embroidered salon logo. Kelly opens the door and I step inside.

"One of your lovely skeins of yarn was left on the winder," I tell her.

The chemical smell inside the salon burns my nose and throat. I wonder if the fumes bother Kelly, or if she's used to it. I hand her the bag, and she peeks inside.

"Thank you for dropping it off. I've been too busy to notice it's missing. I never work this late, but Mrs. Pearson and her husband are leaving for a cruise tomorrow for their forty-fifth wedding anniversary, and this was the only time I could fit her in before she leaves."

Kelly looks toward Mrs. Pearson, who is reclined with her head in the sink. "We want to make sure your hair looks sun-kissed in your vacation photos, don't we, Mrs. Pearson?" Kelly asks in a raised voice so Mrs. Pearson can hear her from inside the sink.

Mrs. Pearson raises a freshly manicured thumb in acknowledgement.

Still looking toward Mrs. Pearson and holding the yarn bag up high enough for Mrs. Pearson to see, Kelly says raising her voice, "I'll be right back to finish taking out your foils, Mrs. Pearson, I just need to run this upstairs to the apartment."

Mrs. Pearson again gives a thumbs-up acknowledgement. Kelly turns to me and wrinkles her nose.

"I don't want to leave it in the salon, it'll absorb the chemical odours," she explains, her voice back to its normal volume.

"I can take it upstairs for you," I offer. "You finish getting Mrs. Pearson's hair cruise-ready, and I'll take the yarn up to your apartment." I smile and take the bag from Kelly's hand.

"Thanks, hun, you're a star. I think Paul is at a meeting somewhere. But, if he's up there, just give him the bag. If not, there's a table on the right, just inside the door. The door should be unlocked." By the time Kelly finishes speaking, she's already back at the sink, her fingers crinkling the foil strips as she removes them from Mrs. Pearson's hair.

I flip the light switch in the small back room. Towels, bottles of shampoo, conditioner and other salon products are organized on floor-to-ceiling shelves along two walls. The back door that leads to the parking lot is in front of me and propped slightly ajar with a unique, heart-shaped grey rock. I assume Kelly opens it so the fresh air can combat the chemical smell in the salon. The stairs are on my left.

At the top of the stairs, muffled voices come

from the apartment. I assume Paul is home and either watching TV or listening to the radio. I sigh, not looking forward to ending my day with another conversation with him.

I knock on the door, hoping he doesn't greet me with a reprimand, lecture, or any other lengthy conversation. My belly is rumbling, and I'm thinking about the leftover lasagna waiting for me in the fridge. I can get home and have it in the microwave within ten minutes of leaving here.

He doesn't answer. I knock again, louder. Still nothing. I put my ear to the door. A TV or radio, but nothing else. Maybe he left the TV on and went out. Or maybe he's asleep.

Tentatively, I turn the doorknob to confirm the door is unlocked. It is. I open the door enough to poke my head inside the apartment.

"Hello?" I call. "Paul? It's Megan. I'm just dropping off some yarn for Kelly."

No response. A sense of chilly apprehension makes a shiver run down my spine. I dismiss my unease, brace myself, and go over my plan. Open the door, step inside, put the yarn on the table. Leave, and tell Kelly on the way out that Paul didn't answer, and the yarn is on the table.

Deep breath.

I open the door slowly and step inside the apartment. There's a table on the right; just like Kelly said. The table has a bowl of keys, two pairs of sunglasses, a wallet, and the bag I handed to Kelly at Knitorious this afternoon. I place the small bag of yarn next to the larger bag, feeling relieved to avoid another unpleasant confrontation with Paul.

I turn to leave and Paul is sitting at the kitchen table. His back is to me. He's slumped forward. I can't see his head; it must be on the kitchen table. What an odd place to fall asleep.

"Hi Paul." I watch to see if he wakes up, or twitches, or something. He doesn't.

With hesitation, I take a step toward the kitchen table.

"Paul?"

No response, no movement.

I attribute the growing knot of anxiety in my stomach to the eerie atmosphere of the apartment and creep toward the kitchen table. I stop and swallow hard when the knot of anxiety rises to my throat. This knot in my stomach is familiar; I feel it whenever something isn't right. It's one way my intuition communicates with me. The knot hasn't been wrong in almost forty years.

I inch closer to Paul. There is something around his neck. Something blue. I squint in case my eyes are playing tricks on me. A skein of yarn? Why would he drape a skein of yarn around his neck? I recognize the yarn; it's a skein of *Breathless*, the same yarn I admired at work today, and the same yarn Kelly bought four skeins of.

The skein is untwisted and draped around Paul's neck like a back-drop necklace, tight in the front with the excess yarn draping down the back of his white undershirt.

I bend to look at his face, except it's immersed in a large bowl. I check for signs of life. He's too still, and his body isn't rising and falling like a body should when it inhales and exhales.

"Paul, I'm going to check your pulse," I tell him.

It's been more than a dozen years since I've had CPR training, but I remember the instructor saying it's important to talk to the person and tell them what you're doing each step of the way.

His hands are on the table, on either side of the large bowl. His cell phone is next to his left hand.

I check his wrist for a pulse. No pulse. He's warmer than room temperature, but not as warm as he should be.

Maybe this just happened. Maybe there's still time to help him.

"Paul, can you hear me? I'm going to lift your head out of the bowl."

Please hear me, Paul. No reaction.

Please be a bizarre household accident or medical episode. Please be all right.

I put one hand on either side of Paul's head, just above his ears, and lift his head from the bowl. It's heavier than I expect. Milk drips from his face into the bowl and onto the table. There are pieces of soggy cereal stuck to his nose and cheek.

He won't be all right.

Paul Sinclair is dead.

CHAPTER 6

THE KNOT in my stomach explodes, shooting panic throughout the rest of my body. My heart thumps double time, banging in my chest like it's trying to escape. With my heartbeat pounding in my ears, and my face flushing with heat, I try to catch my breath and swallow. I have to get help. I have to get out of here.

Should I put his face back in the cereal bowl? Do I move the cereal bowl and lay his head on the table? The CPR course didn't cover this.

How can he be dead? I just saw him this morning, and he was alive. Controlling and bossy, but alive.

Did he drown in a giant bowl of cereal? Was he strangled by the skein of yarn?

I turn his head to the left, and gently rest it on

the bowl, making sure not to submerge it again. I walk backwards toward the door, watching him in case I'm wrong, and he moves.

Please move, Paul! Please wake up!

Groping behind me, I find the door, and back out of the apartment.

Running down the stairs to the salon, I hear myself scream.

"Kelly! Kelly! Call 9-1-1! It's Paul! Something's wrong with Paul!"

Confusion clouds Kelly's face, and she looks like she's in slow motion.

My phone is in my shaky hand, and I call for help.

While I answer the dispatcher's questions, Kelly looks from me to the stairs, then back to me again. I sense she's about to run up to the apartment. Should I spare her from seeing her husband like this? What if it's a crime scene? I position myself between Kelly and the stairs while answering the dispatcher's questions. Kelly wipes her hands on a towel, then sprints to the back room, pushing past me and racing upstairs.

"Paul!" She screams.

I run up the stairs after her. She's kneeling at his side, checking for a pulse. She checks the same wrist I checked moments before. I hope she has a different outcome.

The dispatcher instructs me to unlock the door. I

run downstairs and pass the back door, telling her it's propped open with a rock. I unlock the front door and crack it open to confirm it's unlocked.

Aluminum foil crinkles behind me, and I turn to see Mrs. Pearson on her feet, removing the last of the foils from her hair. She bends forward into the sink and gives her short hair a quick rinse, then while rubbing her wet hair with a towel, walks over to me and tells me that she'll take over door duty. I nod in response.

I stand guard at the back door in case the ambulance pulls up behind the salon. She's still on the line, but the dispatcher stops asking questions. We're silent except for her saying, "Are you still with me, Megan?" at regular intervals, and me responding with, "Yes, I'm here." After which, she says, "Help is almost there." Then, after a brief silence, we do it again.

An ambulance pulls up in front of the Hairway To Heaven, and the lights create a red and blue strobe effect on the walls inside the salon. The dispatcher and I end our call.

In what feels like seconds, the salon is full of first responders. Paramedics, police officers, and firefighters rush around me.

The salon is smaller with all the commotion. To stay out of the way, I find a nearby wall and lean against it, trying to take up as little space as possible.

A police officer leads Kelly down the stairs, and I get her a glass of water from the kitchenette. At least I'm doing something. Anything. I just need to do something useful.

The officer leads Kelly to a chair in front of a sink and helps her sit. I hand her the water and place a box of tissues from the kitchenette on her lap.

A second police officer guides me to a stylist's chair across the room.

I notice a third police officer with Mrs. Pearson at the reception desk.

They're keeping us apart on purpose.

Many years of binge-watching murder mysteries with enthusiasm while I knit has taught me that police keep witnesses at a crime scene apart, so they can interview them separately, and they won't influence each other's statements. People are highly suggestible, particularly when in shock. We can influence each other's recollection of events. For example, if I think something at the crime scene is blue, but I hear another witness describe it as green, I might question my recollection, and convince myself the blue thing was green.

My police officer opens her notepad and starts asking me questions. I fiddle with my wedding ring, now on my right hand, and provide her with my name and contact information. I reach for my wallet to show her my identification.

Adam's voice is inside my head, telling me not to answer any more questions without a lawyer. But I have done nothing wrong, and I have nothing to hide. I decide to cooperate and help any way I can.

She asks me why I'm at the salon and why I went upstairs. She also wants to know how I found Paul, where I touched him, and what else I touched while I was up there. I tell her everything, starting from when Connie and I noticed the skein of yarn Kelly left behind at Knitorious earlier today.

The firefighters leave and more people arrive to take their place. A tall, official-looking man in a suit among them.

My police officer and I both notice the suit, and she excuses herself to speak with him. My experience as an avid viewer of murder mysteries tells me the suit is a police detective.

In the background of my mind, I've been telling myself that Paul had a medical episode, or an accident, and it wasn't murder. I don't want to believe one of my neighbours could be a murder victim. Murders don't happen in my cozy, sweet town. However, a detective's presence makes it difficult to convince myself that either theory explains Paul's death.

If Paul's death is a murder, I was at a murder scene moments after the killer fled. This realization increases my anxiety and leaves a sick taste in my mouth.

Suddenly, I'm hot, my breathing is shallow, I've developed a tremble, and my mouth is too dry. I take deep breaths to bring the trembling under control, but the chemical smell in the salon works against me, so now, on top of everything else, I'm also nauseous. I close my eyes and put my head between my knees.

"Are you all right?" asks an unfamiliar man's voice. "Do you need medical attention?"

I raise my head and try to focus on the suit standing in front of me.

"Would it be possible to step outside for some fresh air?" I gulp, hoping to swallow the wave of nausea rising inside me.

"Of course," he replies, "follow me."

He extends a large, warm hand and helps me up. He leads me to the front door and onto the sidewalk where I inhale as much of the crisp, evening air as my lungs can handle.

"Heavy shoulders, long arms," I mutter to myself.

Heavy shoulders, long arms is a relaxation technique to help release tension from the neck and shoulders. I learned it in a yoga class in my twenties and still use it all these years later.

"Pardon?" the suit asks, looking down at me, and stooping to so he can hear me. "Did you say something?"

I shake my head and lean against the cool brick wall of the salon. I put my hands on my knees and take a few more deep breaths.

Feeling a little less nauseous and shaky, I stand upright. Friends and neighbours line the sidewalk across the street. Police officers and barriers prevent them from coming closer.

A uniformed officer appears and positions himself in front of me, holding up a large white sheet. Is he trying to shield me from seeing the people across the street, or is he trying to shield them from seeing me? Either way, it's too late.

"Someone is getting you a glass of water," the suit informs me.

"Thank you." I look up at him and nod. "I'm feeling better. We can go back inside."

I return to the same chair I was in before, and Mrs. Pearson, followed accompanied by her police escort, hands me a glass of water and rubs my back reassuringly.

This woman is good in a crisis.

Just when I'm feeling like this day will never end, my police officer appears at my side and asks me if there's anyone I can call to pick me up.

My first thought is to call either April or Connie, but it seems silly to ask them to escort me home when I can walk there myself in ten minutes. Also, they'll fuss over me and ask a ton of questions I'm not ready to answer. I'm not prepared to relive this again tonight. I'm tired and hungry. I want to go home and put on my jammies.

I could call Adam. Not for emotional support, but because he's a lawyer. If ever there was a situation where a lawyer might come in handy, this would be it.

I decide not to call anyone. The police officer offers to drive me home, and I accept.

WALKING through my front door reinvigorates me. Five minutes ago, I was exhausted and overwhelmed, and now I'm wide awake and wired. This must be what shock feels like. Tonight I learned that shock is a process with a wide spectrum of reactions ranging from panic, fear, sadness, and nausea, to energetic, hyper, alert, and overwhelmed.

I try to recall something I read once about adrenaline and stressful situations, but can't remember the details.

Adam isn't home yet, and I'm relieved I don't have to answer questions about what happened or sit through reminders about not answering police questions without a lawyer.

I put a piece of lasagna in the microwave. While it warms up, I retrieve my phone from my bag and unlock the screen to see dozens of texts from friends and neighbours wanting to know what's happening, and if everyone is OK.

I reply to April and Connie first, letting them know Kelly, Mrs. Pearson, and I are OK, but Paul isn't. I also tell them I need a few hours to process everything, and I'll talk to them tomorrow. They offer to come over and promise not to ask questions. I appreciate it, but thank them and decline. Right now, I want to be alone and end this long, awful day.

Scrolling through my missed messages, Adam texted to say I shouldn't wait up, and he'll be around in the morning to talk.

I text him back and tell him Paul is dead, and the town is in shock. He'll find out anyway, so it may as well be from me. I don't tell him I was the one who found him or it looks like murder. I'm not ready to deal with questions yet.

He doesn't respond.

It's much later than I normally eat dinner, but I haven't eaten since this morning, and I'm famished and nauseous at the same time. As a result, I eat my lasagna faster than I should, and hope I won't be up all night with indigestion.

I put my dishes in the dishwasher and make a mug of chamomile tea while I finish scrolling through the missed text messages.

In bed, I toss and turn. My body is exhausted,

but my brain refuses to yield to its demand for sleep. When I close my eyes and try to be still, I relive it. Paul hunched over the table. Kelly sprinting for the stairs. The chemical odour in the salon. Milk dripping off Paul's nose and the pieces of cereal stuck to his face. His not-quite-warm-enough skin. It plays over and over in my head, a movie I can't pause.

To distract myself, I turn on the TV and find a channel that only airs 1990s sitcoms. I leave it on until I either fall asleep, or it's time to get up.

With the theme song from Friends filling my bedroom, I close my eyes and take deep breaths.

CHAPTER 7

WEDNESDAY, September 11th

I wake up to Paul and Jamie Buchman arguing about a pretty nurse on Mad About You. Sleep was elusive and occupied by a dream that had me running around the edge of a huge fountain of cereal, trying not to fall in while a giant skein of blue yarn chased me.

I turn off the TV, hurry through my morning routine, and rush out the door.

Adam's car isn't in the driveway. His briefcase, shoes, and coat aren't where he leaves them, so I assume he didn't come home last night.

I walk into town in case Water Street is still closed in front of Hairway to Heaven. Also, I'm too tired to drive.

When I round the corner onto Water Street,

yellow crime scene tape glistens in the light of the dawning sun and wafts in the breeze. I cross the street because the police officer stationed in front of Hairway To Heaven is blocking the sidewalk.

There are fewer bystanders this morning, but still a good-sized crowd. As I thread my way through clusters of curious onlookers, someone calls my name. I stretch my neck and scan the crowd, my gaze landing on April who's waving me over to her and Connie.

They envelop me in a group hug.

"How did you sleep, my dear?" Connie squeezes my shoulder with one arm and hands me a coffee with the other.

"Thank you!" I say, accepting the coffee and holding it under my nose before I take a sip. It's hazelnut-French vanilla medium roast, and right now, it's my favourite coffee in the world.

April leans in and whispers in my ear, "Phillip was here early to receive a delivery, and he saw Kelly. She got in the back of a police car and they drove her away."

Phillip Wilde owns Wilde Flowers, the florist shop next to Knitorious. He also lives next door to me; we're neighbours at work and at home.

"Poor Kelly," I say.

I thought my night was bad. I can't imagine what she's going through.

People notice me, and word of my presence

makes its way through the crowd. Soon, people are approaching me to ask how I'm doing. Some people are sincere, some are trying to find out what I know, and the rest fall into both categories.

In light of the attention, Connie suggests we make our way to Knitorious, and we walk away from the crowd.

I'm not trying to avoid answering my friends' and neighbours' questions, I'm just not sure what I should and shouldn't say. I want to respect Kelly's privacy and the police investigation, but Harmony Lake is a small, tight-knit community, and a tragedy like this affects all of us.

After we've put some distance between us and the crowd, April asks if anyone official declared Paul's death a murder.

"I don't know," I reply. "I answered a lot of questions last night, but I didn't ask any. It didn't look like he passed away peacefully in his sleep, but it also didn't look like a gruesome murder scene."

This is the most I've said to anyone other than the police.

"Not all murders are gruesome, my dear," Connie reminds me. "Look at those murder mystery shows set in quaint British villages, they're never messy."

Connie shares my enthusiasm for murder

mysteries. We're both experienced armchair investigators.

INSIDE THE STORE, I lock the door behind us. We don't open for two hours, and I'm not ready to deal with people.

Connie excuses herself and goes up to her apartment for a shower, while April and I sit in the cozy sitting area sipping our coffees. Harlow runs into the store, jumps onto the sofa, and nestles into April's hip, settling in for his early morning nap.

"I know Paul was a bully and rubbed many people the wrong way, but someone would have to hate him a lot to kill him," April speculates as she absentmindedly strokes Harlow. "Especially with his wife in the same building. I mean, they risked being caught by Kelly unless they entered the apartment from the roof."

"If they were already in the apartment when Paul got home, they only risked being seen when they left," I point out.

I fiddle with my ring, still getting used to wearing it on my right hand.

"Either the killer knew Kelly was working late in the salon and Paul was alone in the apartment, or they intended to kill both of them, but Kelly wasn't there, so they settled for only killing Paul," she theorizes.

"I wonder if Mr. and Mrs. Pearson left for their cruise?" I wonder out loud.

"You mentioned her last night in your text, but we didn't see her there. I don't think anyone saw her, and other than you, no one else has mentioned her," April says.

"She was the client Kelly stayed late for. No one else knows that?"

"No. We only knew you were there because you came outside for air. The police held up sheets to block the view when anything, or I guess anyone, left the salon."

April leaves for Artsy Tartsy, where she'll work behind the counter while Tamara works her magic in the kitchen.

Alone with my thoughts, my mind replays last night's events on a constant loop, and I worry I missed something important, or compromised the crime scene when I found Paul and tried to help him. Maybe I shouldn't have lifted his head and put it in a different position.

Harlow wakes up and meows loudly at me.

"I know what you want, handsome. You only ever want one thing." I pick him up, carry him to the kitchenette and put him on the floor. He weaves in and out of my ankles while I spoon his breakfast into a dish and place it on the floor in front of him.

When I walk back into the store, Adam is outside waving at me through the window. I let him in.

"I knocked, but I guess you didn't hear it in the back."

He's wearing a suit. Either he's on his way to the office, or on his way home. We sit on the sofa, and he tells me he didn't get my text about Paul's death until this morning. I fill him in.

"You were dropping off yarn?" Adam asks, stunned. "I assumed you went there because Paul was blackmailing me. He's the person who told you about Stephanie Murphy and gave you the screenshots, right?"

"No!" I reply, confused. "Fred Murphy gave me the photos, not Paul," I clarify. "Paul knew about you and Stephanie? How? And how did he get the photos?" I take a breath and let sink in that Paul had the photos. "Paul was blackmailing us?" I ask. "In *addition* to Fred and Stephanie Murphy? Or did they all work together?" I shake my head as though it will help the pieces fall into place and everything will suddenly make sense. "Was there one blackmail scheme or two? I'm so confused."

Seriously, what's going on? I might need a chart or something.

Adam brings his hands together in front of his chest.

"You spoke with Fred?" he asks, then points to

me. I nod. "Fred told you about Stephanie and me, and gave you the photos?" He points again and I nod again. "OK, Fred and Stephanie Murphy blackmailed me to leave the firm. Then, Paul contacted me yesterday morning and told me to transfer a certain amount of money into his account by noon. He said if I didn't do it, he would send the photos to you," Adam explains. "There's no way I would give in to Paul's demand. I didn't send him any money. I tried calling and texting you, but you didn't answer. Then you texted me the photo, so I assumed when I didn't pay him, Paul followed through with his threat and told you about Stephanie."

This explains why Paul wanted to talk to me yesterday.

"How did Paul get the photos you sent to Stephanie?"

"I have no idea," Adam replies with a one-shoulder shrug.

"I saw Paul and Fred together yesterday," I tell him. "They were arguing in a car outside Artsy Tartsy. I assumed Fred parked wrong, or didn't use his blinker, or some such thing. But maybe they knew each other and were discussing blackmail."

Adam leans toward me and rests his elbows on his knees.

"Meg, the texts and the photos on Paul's phone, and his text conversation with me, give us motive to kill him. The police will want to question us. Soon."

"Where were you last night?" I probe. "The police will want to know."

He didn't come home, and I assume he wasn't with his blackmailer-girlfriend, Stephanie Murphy.

"A hotel near the office," Adam explains. "The firm keeps a courtesy suite." He sighs. "I resigned yesterday. Effective today. I stayed late tying up loose ends. It was late when I left, and I was too tired to drive home, so I stayed at the hotel."

Wow. He left the firm! This is the end of an era. Under normal circumstances, this would be a monumental event, but considering everything that's happened since yesterday, it seems almost insignificant.

I want to ask him if this affair with a married woman that cost him his job, and got us blackmailed twice over, was worth it. But I bite my tongue. We need calm, level heads, not heated arguments and accusations.

The floorboards creak when Connie descends the stairs. Adam stands up, smooths his tie, smiles, and walks toward her to greet her as she enters the store.

Adam is a dangerous combination of handsome and charming, packaged in a well-tailored, expensive suit. He looks at you like you're the only person in his world.

Even Connie isn't immune to his charm. As he takes her hands and kisses her cheek, his charisma draws her in like a moth to a flame. He compliments her perfume and still holding her hands, tells her how beautiful she looks in blue because it brings out her blue eyes. She blushes like a schoolgirl. He can't help it. He doesn't know he's doing it. It's not predatory, he's sincere and means everything he says. It's just how he is. He's oblivious to the effect he has on people, particularly women, and his naivete is part of his charm.

They're talking about Paul and how his death shocked the community. Adam doesn't mention Paul was blackmailing us.

He throws a few more compliments at Connie, then goes home to shower and change, leaving Connie and I alone in the quiet store. Except for Harlow purring and the gentle clickity-clack of our needles, we knit in silence until it's time to open the store.

"It's showtime." Connie smiles at me, puts her knitting on the table and gets up to unlock the door and flip the CLOSED sign to OPEN.

CHAPTER 8

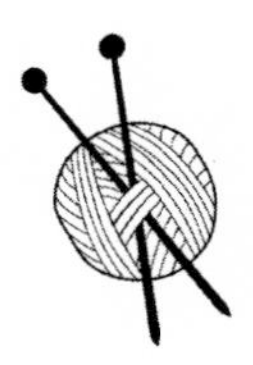

WATER STREET IS busy for a typical Wednesday. But today isn't a typical Wednesday; it's the day after our neighbour was killed in his home.

People stroll along Water Street, meandering in and out of stores. They're trying to make sense of what happened. They find comfort in reassuring each other and not being alone today.

As shocked people wander in and out of Knitorious, Harlow makes himself available to provide comfort, accept rubs, and takes on the role of self-appointed emotional support animal.

Almost everyone asks me what I saw yesterday. The few who don't ask me themselves hover nearby so they can hear what I say. I tell them I can't talk about it until the police tell me otherwise. Word must have spread that I'm not talking because, by lunchtime, fewer people ask me about it.

Connie and I take turns having lunch. When it's my turn, I go upstairs to her apartment and have a sandwich she made for me. I rarely take a full lunch break. Usually, I'm content to eat in the kitchenette then go back to work. Today I take my time and use the full hour.

I return from lunch to find Connie dangling a shimmery pom-pom on a string in front of Harlow.

"Will you be all right if I leave for my appointment, my dear?"

I forgot about Connie's appointment today. She mentioned it yesterday before I went to Hairway To Heaven.

"Of course!" I say, "You go. I'll be fine. Besides, Stitch-Fix is this afternoon, so I'll be busy and the afternoon will fly by."

Stitch-Fix is a knitting clinic we host one afternoon each week where knitters bring in their knitting problems and mistakes, and Connie and I help fix them. I love the challenge.

"Only if you're sure. I don't mind rescheduling. I meant to reschedule this morning, but in all the excitement I forgot." She shrugs, chuckling at her forgetfulness.

"I'll be fine," I tell her, again.

She leaves through the back door, and for the first time today, the store is empty. I tidy the shelves and return mislaid skeins of yarn where they belong.

In the bulky yarn section, I stare at the remaining skeins of Breathless. A now-familiar wave of nausea washes over me and in my mind's eye I see this yarn wrapped around Paul's neck with him hunched over the kitchen table. The yarn dangling down the back of his white undershirt. I decide I'll remove Breathless from the shelf. Out of sight, out of mind, and all that.

While contemplating which yarn to put in its place, the bell over the door jingles. A tall, fortyish-year-old man in a suit looks around. He's familiar, but I can't place him. He's not our usual demographic. If he was a return customer, I'd remember him for sure.

We make eye contact and walk toward each other, meeting at the harvest table.

"Hi," I say, smiling.

"Hello, again," he responds, also smiling.

He extends a hand and offers me a business card:

Detective Sergeant Eric Sloane
Ontario Provincial Police

He's the suit from the salon last night.

"Of course!" I exclaim. "You're the detective from Hairway to Heaven!"

I extend my hand, we shake, and I gesture for him to have a seat at the harvest table.

"Why the OPP?" I ask. "Isn't the Harmony Lake Police Department investigating?"

The OPP is what the locals call the Ontario Provincial Police.

"Harmony Lake PD doesn't have a major crimes division, so they asked us to assist," he explains. "Apparently, there isn't enough crime in Harmony Lake to warrant a major crimes division."

"Not until yesterday," I confirm.

It's true. Compared to bigger towns and cities, Harmony Lake has a low crime rate. We have our share of parking tickets, jaywalkers, and the occasional drunk-in-public tourist. A few years back, there was a spate of wallet robberies, but we've never had a murder. Until now.

Eric Sloane smells good. Like a forest after it rains. I didn't notice yesterday with everything else going on. And not to be shallow, but he's hot. If you're into tall men with dark hair, brown eyes with flecks of gold, and friendly smiles.

Don't stare, Megan.

"How are you?" he asks. "I know yesterday was a shock. You weren't feeling well at the salon last night. Are you feeling better?"

"It was a shock, for sure, but I feel better today," I reply. "Thank you for asking. I've been thinking about Kelly. How is she doing?"

"She has family with her, and we're making sure

she has access to all available resources to help her."

It's amazing how well he answered my question without actually answering my question.

"Well, please tell her everyone is thinking of her and sending her lots of love and support."

I doubt he'll say those exact words, but hopefully he'll relay the sentiment.

"How can I help you, Detective Sergeant?"

"Please, call me Eric."

"Only if you call me Megan."

Eric pulls a small notebook and pen from his breast pocket, and I notice his nice hands. You know, if you're into large, powerful hands with clean, well-groomed nails.

Don't stare at his hands, Megan. Breathe. Act normal.

"Can you tell me about the yarn that Ms. Sinclair purchased yesterday?"

He finds a blank page in his notebook, and pen in hand, is poised to write.

"Sure."

I walk over to the shelf and pick up a skein of Breathless. I return to my seat and place the skein between us.

He asks me how many skeins she purchased, if they were the same, and if she purchased anything else. I print a copy of her receipt and give it to him so he can see the transaction details.

"Other than the yarn, did Ms. Sinclair leave anything else behind yesterday?"

"Nope," I reply, shaking my head. "Just the yarn I dropped off."

"Are you sure she left the store with everything else, including the knitting needles?"

"Yes. I put them in the bag myself. She definitely had the needles when she left."

"Did she have both needles? Could she have left one knitting needle behind?"

I retrieve a pair of needles identical to the ones Kelly purchased, return to my seat, and place the needles on the table between us, beside the skein of yarn.

"They're packaged together," I explain. "To lose one, the packaging would have to rip or tear in two spots. Connie handed me the needles, I rang them up, and put them in the bag. One of us would have noticed if the packaging was torn to that extent. Connie wouldn't have them on the rack if they were torn, never mind sell them."

He nods and makes a note. I try to read it, but his penmanship is messy. It's also small, and from my vantage point, upside down. I can only decipher the date at the top of the page.

"Can you tell me about the altercation you and Ms. Shaw had with Paul Sinclair yesterday at the park?"

He stares at me, gauging my reaction.

"Hmmm... I wouldn't call it an altercation." I shake my head. "It was a typical interaction with Paul. If it was an altercation, every interaction Paul ever had was an altercation. I missed a committee meeting yesterday morning at the Animal Centre, and Paul chased me through the park to reprimand me. He wouldn't let it go, so April—er, Ms. Shaw—told him to back off." I shrug. "Then we left."

He scrawls another note, then looks at me again.

"Why did you miss the meeting at the Animal Centre?"

I take a deep breath and let it out.

"My husband's girlfriend's husband texted me and asked to meet." *Good luck connecting those dots, Eric!* "This is a new situation," I explain. "It distracted me, and derailed my morning," I explain.

He nods and writes in his book.

Harlow jumps onto the table, nudges Eric's pen, and steps onto the page Eric is writing on. Eric stops writing; Harlow doesn't give him much choice. He scratches Harlow between the ears, and Harlow flops onto the notebook, purring contentedly.

"I need to ask you some more questions, Megan. Can we meet again so I can take a full statement?"

My heart thumps double-time in my chest, and I swallow hard.

"Am I a suspect?"

CHAPTER 9

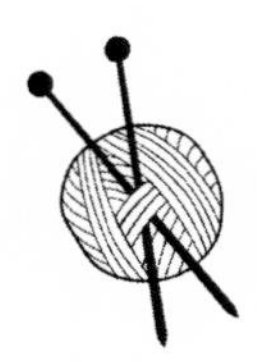

My heart and stomach switch places while I wait for Eric's response.

"Everyone is a suspect until they're eliminated, Megan, and your statement will help to eliminate you."

Again, he answers my question without actually answering my question. This must be a skill cops learn at the police academy.

"I didn't do it," I insist, panicking. "I'd never hurt anybody, never mind kill them. Besides, I don't think I'm strong enough to strangle someone, even with a skein of yarn."

"Hold on." Eric raises his right hand in a stop gesture. "Why did you say that, about the yarn? Why do you think that's how Mr. Sinclair died?"

"I found him, remember?" I remind him. "I

saw the yarn around his neck. Also, if he died of natural causes, or an accident, I doubt you'd be here. Based on what I saw, he either drowned in a giant bowl of cereal or was strangled with a skein of yarn and fell forward into the cereal. It would be weird to eat cereal while wearing a yarn-necklace. And if he *was* wearing a yarn necklace, it wouldn't have been pulled tight against the front of his throat. Therefore, I assume the killer strangled Paul from behind, then left his face in the bowl."

I stop incriminating myself long enough to take a breath. To Eric, it must sound like I just confessed to killing Paul by strangling him with yarn and letting his face fall into a huge bowl of cereal.

Now I understand why Adam is so keen on people having a lawyer present when they talk to the police.

The bell above the door jingles. Harlow jumps down to greet the new arrival.

Eric closes his notebook, clicks his pen, and returns them to his breast pocket. He pushes the skein of yarn and needles aside and places his hands palms down on the table between us.

"Megan, can you do me a favour please? Don't tell anyone else what you just told me. Can you please keep it to yourself?"

Terrified, I nod. If I wasn't a suspect before, I am now. Why didn't I stop myself from talking myself all the way to the top of Eric's suspect list? What was I thinking?

"I think someone's here for Stitch-Fix." I stand up and push my chair in.

At the front of the store, a scowling knitter holds a partially completed blanket with a large hole in it. I greet her, smile knowingly at her blanket, and tell her I'll be right back to help her with her knitting problem.

I walk Eric to the door. We agree to meet tomorrow, so I can give him a statement and answer more questions. He says he'll be in touch in the morning to arrange a time.

After he leaves, I shudder. Paul was murdered. There's a murderer in our midst. If it were tourist season, we could blame an outsider for what happened, but the summer tourist season is over and the winter tourist season hasn't begun, which means a local murdered Paul. One of my neighbours is a killer.

I WISH the last Stitch-Fix knitter a good day after helping her close a hole in a sweater sleeve made when she accidentally created a stitch about sixty rows ago. My tummy rumbles and I head to the kitchenette for a snack. I'm opening the fridge when the door jingles. I poke my head into the store and see April carrying one of my favourite things, a white confectionery box with the Artsy Tartsy logo on the lid. I grab two glasses of water and join her on the sofa.

She opens the box and reveals warm pumpkin oatmeal cookies for us, and a small container of whipped cream for Harlow.

While we enjoy our treats, I tell April about Eric Sloane's visit and my theory about the killer being local, and possibly someone we know and see all the time.

"In books and on TV, the killer is almost always the spouse," April comments. "I mean, Kelly had access to him, and it was her yarn that killed him."

What did she just say? She knows about the yarn?

"You know how Paul died?"

"It was in the WSBA group chat." April shrugs and picks up another cookie. "Mort mentioned it to someone. He said the coroner had to be careful when he removed Paul to not disturb the yarn around his neck. Whoever he told mentioned it to someone in the group chat and now the entire WSBA knows."

Which means the entire town knows. The Water Street Business Association (WSBA) group chat is for members only. I'm not a member, but Connie and April are members because they own businesses on Water Street. They use the chat for things like announcing sales, reminders about meetings, and gossip.

Mort Ackerman is our local funeral director. He owns Mourning Glory Funeral Home in Harmony Hills.

I make a mental note to text Eric and tell him the thing he wants me to keep to myself is common knowledge, and make it clear I didn't let the yarn out of the bag, so to speak.

"Kelly had to leave Mrs. Pearson long enough to go upstairs, kill Paul, compose herself, and come back downstairs. When I got there, she was her usual, friendly, laid-back self. There was no hint she just killed her husband," I reason.

"She would be composed if she's a psychopath," April deduces. "Psychopaths don't lose their composure after they kill. And they can act normal, that's how they trick the rest of us into believing they aren't psychopaths."

The thought of a psychopathic killer roaming the streets of our community weirds us out.

I take the last cookie and offer it to April, but she waves it away. I break it in half, offer her half, but she waves it off, too, so it's all mine!

"I saw Paul and Fred in a car together when I left the bakery yesterday. They were arguing. I'm not sure if they already knew each other, or if Paul caught him breaking a bylaw and confronted him."

"That's interesting…" She nods, her gaze wandering to the left.

"Paul had an issue with Ryan too..." I say with my mouth full. These cookies are so good, I forget my manners. I raise my right index finger until I swallow the cookie. "Something must have happened between."

"Paul had issues with lots of people, and lots of people had issues with him. If having an issue with Paul gets your name added to the suspect list, almost everyone in town is on the list."

She makes a good point.

"Speaking of issues with Paul," I say, "I'm pretty sure Adam and I are at the top of the suspect list."

I take a deep breath and tell April about Paul having the photos and using them to try to blackmail Adam.

Before she can react, we're interrupted by the jingle of the front door, and Connie swoops in and joins us. We fill her in until it's time to lock the door and flip the sign to CLOSED.

CHAPTER 10

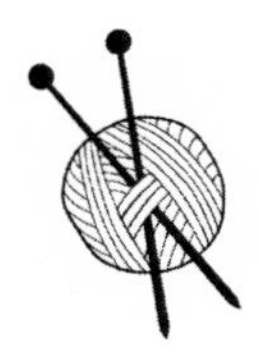

As soon as I walk in the house, I text Hannah and ask her to FaceTime.

Adam isn't home, and I know he'd want to be here when I tell her about Paul, but April and I agreed we need to tell our daughters tonight about Paul's murder. We agreed to FaceTime our respective daughters as soon as we get home. This way they'll hear it from us instead of from each other, a friend in Harmony Lake, or a social media post.

I hit Send on my text to Hannah, then pull out Eric's business card and fire off a text explaining the information he asked me to keep to myself is all over town because of someone else. I don't tell him it was Mort because, first; I don't know for sure it *was* Mort, I only know what April told me she read in the WSBA group chat, and second, Eric is a detective. He can use his detective skills to figure it out.

Hannah calls me on FaceTime, and I tell her about Paul. A few minutes into our conversation, the doorbell rings. I look through the living room window. Eric Sloane is standing on the porch. Two visits in one day. Lucky me. I open the door and gesture for him to come in as I say goodbye and I love you to Hannah and end our chat.

"I sent you a text," I say, leading Eric into the living room.

We sit, I offer him a beverage, and he declines.

"I was driving, but I read it when I pulled into your driveway. It's difficult to keep things under wraps in a town this small. The yarn was a hold-back, but it's all right."

"What's a hold-back?" I ask.

Eric explains that a hold-back is evidence or information from the crime scene that only the killer would know about. The hold-back is useful when interrogating a suspect. If they mention the hold-back, it's a good sign they were there. A hold-back can also eliminate someone who confesses to a crime they didn't commit, because according to Eric, people actually do that. If they don't mention the hold-back, it's less likely they were at the crime scene when the crime occurred.

"I'm hoping to see Mr. Martel," he says.

Relief washes over me, followed by guilt about feeling relieved because he wants to question Adam instead of me.

"He's not here," I tell Eric. "I can text him, let him know you're here and ask when he'll be back?"

Eric nods, "Thanks, that would be great."

I text Adam and wait for a reply.

"Do you have any idea where he might be?" Eric asks.

This is a loaded question. I'm pretty sure Eric figured out Adam and I aren't an example of matrimonial bliss. Telling him I met with my husband's girlfriend's husband was a big clue, and so are the photos and texts between Adam and Stephanie that Eric would have found on Paul's phone. I sense he's looking for me to clarify our marital status and give him some back story without coming out and asking me.

"We still live under the same roof, but Adam and I separated months ago. I don't know where he is, and we don't monitor each other's comings and goings." That's the short version.

"Was the separation triggered by the photos on Mr. Sinclair's phone?"

He asks carefully, trying to be sensitive to the situation which I appreciate.

"No." I shake my head. "As far as I know, Adam's affair with Stephanie is recent. I found out about it yesterday from Fred. He and Stephanie threatened to make the photos public if Adam didn't leave the firm. I found out Paul had the photos this morning when Adam told me. I swear I didn't know Paul was blackmailing Adam when I went to the salon yesterday." My phone dings. "It's Adam. He says he's only a few minutes away."

"That's great. Thank you," Eric responds. "Is it possible Mr. Martel's desire to keep the affair secret made him do something drastic?"

"No!" I answer quickly and emphatically, hoping to convince Eric that Adam didn't kill Paul. "Adam wouldn't hurt a soul. He takes spiders outside instead of killing them, and in the winter, he puts them in the garage instead of outside, so they won't freeze," I explain.

"But spiders weren't blackmailing him, Megan."

"Adam is a smart man and an excellent lawyer," I reason. "He knows eliminating Paul wouldn't eliminate the evidence that Paul blackmailed him. At the very least, he would have taken Paul's phone with him and disposed of it or deleted the evidence to slow down the investigation. But Paul's phone was on the table with the yarn, I saw it. I doubt the contents of his phone were the only motive for Paul's murder."

"You're very observant," Eric comments, looking impressed. "Have Mr. Martel and Ms. Sinclair ever had an intimate relationship?"

Excuse me? Did he just suggest Adam and Kelly are having an affair? Why would he ask me this? Adam and Kelly? Do they even know each other? Adam gets his hair cut by a barber in the city. He's always at work and hardly ever in town. How many women has Adam been seeing? Does he send these intimate photos to all of them?

Speechless, I hope the look on my face convinces Eric this is news to me.

"Are they?" I ask in a barely audible whisper. "Having an affair, I mean?"

"We found communication between them, and evidence they've met face-to-face. What do you know about that?"

Searching for words, I shake my head. Did Eric blindside me on purpose? It makes me feel like I can't trust him.

We both turn toward the door when it opens. Adam walks in with a laptop box under his arm. He slips his shoes off and walks past us and into the dining room where he places the box on the dining room table.

Adam greets us, then he and Eric introduce themselves and shake hands.

Would Adam like to go to the police station? Or would he like to talk here and I can go out? They look to me for an answer, but I'm still speechless and processing the bombshell about Adam and Kelly. All I can do is shake my head and shrug.

Adam opts for the police station and puts on his shoes. Eric joins Adam at the door with one hand on the doorknob.

"Thank you, Megan." Eric smiles.

I nod in response. His smile offends me; it's like he's pleased with himself for playing head games with me.

"Lock the door behind me and don't wait up," Adam says.

He smiles and closes the door behind him. I lock it, even though we never lock the door when one of us is home. Everything has changed so much in 24 hours.

Adam and Kelly having an affair? It doesn't feel right. Yesterday, my instincts told me Fred was telling the truth about our spouses. Today, my instincts tell me the opposite; if there is a relationship between Adam and Kelly, it's not an intimate one. Too bad instincts aren't evidence.

If Adam and Kelly were having an affair, it gives Kelly a motive to kill Paul. Maybe Paul found out and was planning to leave her. Or maybe she wanted to leave him for Adam, but Paul made it difficult. Maybe murder is less expensive and faster than divorce. Maybe Paul blackmailed her too.

Kelly is always so sweet and kind to me. Could she be sleeping with my husband and still act totally normal around me?

April would say, yes, she could, if she's a psychopath.

An affair with Kelly would give Adam another motive too. Maybe Paul threatened to tell Kelly about Stephanie, his other mistress. Or maybe Paul wouldn't go quietly and let Adam and Kelly to be together.

All this what-iffing makes my head hurt. In the kitchen, I pour myself a small glass of wine. My phone dings.

Connie: According to the WSBA group chat, Kelly left the police station. She's staying with her sister in the city. She can't go home because the apartment and salon are still crime scenes.

Why would she want to? Paul has been dead for twenty-four hours. If I were Kelly, the murder scene is the last place I'd want to go.

Ding! This time it's April. It's a group text to Connie and me.

April: Did you guys hear Kelly is staying with her sister?

Connie: Yes, that poor girl! At least she has her sister!

Me: Eric and Adam just went to the police station. Eric hinted that Adam and Kelly are having or have had an affair.

April: ?!?!?!

Connie: Oh my!

April: Maybe he's speculating?

Connie: I was about to say that!

Connie's exclamation points are the text-equivalent of speaking with her hands, and it makes me smile. We text for a while longer, until I decide to get ready for bed.

CHAPTER 11

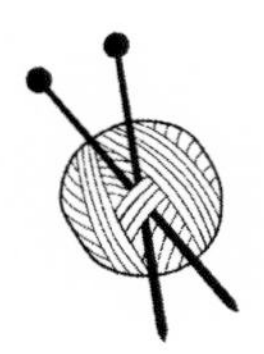

THURSDAY, September 12th

On my walk to work through the drizzle and fog, I stop at Latte Da and pick up two café mochas with whipped cream.

At Knitorious, I stop to turn on the computer then hang up my jacket. I leave Connie's coffee on the counter in the kitchenette for her to find when she comes downstairs.

I only work a half-day today. I want to pack the online orders and drop them off at the post office when I leave at lunchtime.

Tending to the technology-related tasks at Knitorious is my job because Connie claims she doesn't like technology. Despite her insistence that she hates it, she's a proficient texter and user of social media. But given the choice, she'd prefer ledger books and checklists to keep track of the accounts and manage inventory. Administrative tasks are one of my happy places; I majored in economics and minored in accounting. I like being in charge of the behind-the-scenes organization.

I print the online orders and walk from shelf to shelf, collecting the yarn and notions to fill them. Then, I pull out tissue paper, envelopes, and bubble mailers from under the counter. The crinkling of the tissue paper lures Harlow like a beacon to the harvest table where I'm working. He loves tissue paper, so I ball-up a couple of sheets for him to play with, and toss them onto the floor, at the opposite end of the store. He chases and attacks them a safe distance from the sheets I'm using to pack the yarn; I'm sure customers would prefer their yarn to arrive free of cat fur.

While I wrap, pack, and label, my phone dings. Eric wants to know what time we can meet. I'll text him later; I want to finish up and put everything away before Harlow loses interest in his tissue paper balls and helps me.

Also, I'm not eager to talk to Eric. I'm still bitter about how he dropped the Adam-and-Kelly bombshell with no regard for my feelings and seemed to take pride in shocking me.

Connie is puttering around in the kitchenette. It's Thursday, so I assume she's cleaning out the fridge and checking our supplies of coffee, tea, snacks, cat food, and such.

"What the...? Oh, my."

"Is everything all right, Connie?" I shout without losing my rhythm, packing and addressing bubble mailers.

Connie comes into the store holding a thingamajig in her hand.

"I opened the dishwasher to empty it and this," —she holds the offending thingamajig in front of her nose—"was sitting in the bottom and is probably the reason the dishes are still dirty."

"I'm sure The Wright Men can fix it. Ryan's van was on Water Street when I was walking to work. If he's still around, maybe he can fix it today, and maybe I can ask him some questions while he's here."

"Ask him a few questions about what, my dear?"

"About Paul not trusting Ryan and not wanting him in the salon or the store. Right now, Adam and I are pretty high on the suspect list, and if I can find the real killer, I can clear our names."

"Are you suggesting that Ryan Wright killed Paul?"

Connie sounds incredulous, and I get it. Ryan is one of the last people I'd ever suspect of murder. But on TV, the killer is always the last person everyone suspects.

"No," I reply, "but maybe whatever happened between them will shed some light on what happened to Paul."

Connie picks up the landline and calls Ryan. He's servicing the walk-in cooler next door at Wilde Flowers and says he can look at the dishwasher in about an hour. I finish packing orders while Connie returns to the kitchenette and hand-washes the dishes.

AN HOUR LATER, on the nose, Ryan knocks at the back door. I open the door and Ryan and his toolbox get straight to work assessing the dishwasher situation. I hand him the thingamajig we think is causing the problem, and Harlow and I hover around him while Connie serves the handful of customers milling around the store.

Harlow rubs against Ryan's ankles while he and I talk about Paul's murder and how shocked we were. I ask him if he's heard any rumours. He visits so many homes and businesses each day, he must hear things.

He says he's heard nothing other than sympathy for Kelly. The consensus is that it was a targeted murder by someone Paul disagreed with, not a random attack or serial killer.

"Are you one of the people Paul disagreed with?" I ask, trying to be delicate.

He doesn't seem fazed by my question and continues tightening, or loosening, I can't tell the difference, the thing he's either tightening or loosening, without losing his rhythm.

"Now, why would you ask me that, Megan?"

"The day Paul died, Kelly mentioned Paul wouldn't let her hire The Wright Men For The Job anymore. He told her he didn't trust you."

Ryan stops working and pops his head out from inside the dishwasher.

"If anyone isn't trustworthy, it's Paul." He places the tool he was using back in the toolbox and pulls out a different tool. "Six weeks ago, Paul offered to pay me to burglarize Hairway To Heaven."

Ryan pauses while I take in what he said. I'm taken aback and need a few seconds to catch up.

"Why would he want to steal from his wife's business? What did he want you to steal? Shampoo and conditioner?" I ask, spinning my ring.

"Kelly's invested in new equipment this year. New computers, new styling tools, and other stuff that Paul said wasn't cheap. He said he'd keep Kelly away from the salon overnight and give me a list. I'd steal the items on the list and deliver them to a buyer he lined up. I'd collect the cash from the buyer, give half to Paul, and keep the other half for my trouble. He insisted it wasn't stealing because they insure everything, so Kelly could file an insurance claim and replace it."

Theft *and* insurance fraud. That's a big job to ask your local handyperson to do.

"What did you tell him?" I ask.

Ryan chuckles. "I told him no way. But Paul didn't like my answer. He said if I didn't do it, he'd tell everyone I'm a felon."

I close the door to the kitchenette. In Harmony Lake, all walls have ears.

"Are you a felon, Ryan?" I ask in a whisper.

"Technically, yes," he replies matter-of-factly. "Remember about five years ago when I moved to Ottawa to work for my Uncle's construction company?"

I nod.

"Well, I wasn't in a good place then. I made some poor decisions. I discovered some guys on the site were stealing copper wire, and other things, and reselling it. They offered to cut me in if I didn't rat them out. I accepted. For the next few months, they stole from worksites, and I pretended not to notice. Once a week a guy would bring me a coffee from the coffee truck, but it was an empty cup filled with cash. I didn't know one of them was an undercover cop who infiltrated the group to bring down the theft ring. When they busted us, they charged me along with everyone else. I copped a plea and spent three months in jail."

"Wow, Ryan. I had no idea. How did Paul know? Did you tell him?"

"After my release, I was on probation. For three years, I drove into the city to visit my probation officer. Paul saw me go into the probation office and snooped around." Ryan shakes his head. "He was probably in the city visiting the casino," he mumbles.

Ryan ducks his head into the dishwasher and continues working.

It seems Paul had a habit of blackmailing people. First Adam, and now Ryan. Maybe that's why he and Fred argued in the car. Maybe Paul blackmailed the Murphys too. But how did he know Adam was seeing Stephanie Murphy? Did he see them together, like he saw Ryan in the city?

"How did you avoid being blackmailed? I mean, Paul didn't tell anyone, right?"

Ryan's head pops out of the dishwasher again.

"Paul likes to gamble. It used to be a big problem for him, but he learned to control it after Kelly threatened to leave him if he didn't. Lately, his gambling problem hasn't been under control. He borrowed money to hide his gambling debt from Kelly. I told Paul I know about his gambling habit and debt and threatened to tell Kelly about it, tell her about his plan to rob the salon." Ryan shrugs. "He stopped talking to me. It sounds like he lied to Kelly to make sure she wouldn't talk to me either."

"How do you know about Paul's gambling debt?"

"I do a lot of work for Jay Singh. He's a money lender who lives in Harmony Hills. We're friends. He's super smart, so when Paul tried to blackmail me, I asked Jay for advice. Jay told me he loaned Paul money to pay off his gambling debt, and Paul was behind making the repayments. He told me to use the information to get away from Paul. He said he also hoped it would pressure Paul into getting his payments up to date. And before you ask, I was with Jay when Paul died. He hired me to assemble a backyard play set for his twins."

Ryan's head and shoulders disappear into the dishwasher. I open the door and return to the store.

Ryan replaces the thingamajig and puts the dishwasher back together. Then he gives Connie an invoice, which she pays out of the till, and leaves.

WHEN CONNIE and I are alone, I disclose to her what Ryan told me. I know she'll keep Ryan's past to herself. She isn't as shocked as I expected about Ryan's criminal past, but she shares my shock about Paul's scheme to burgle the salon.

This means people without the last name Martel had a motive to kill Paul.

If Hairway To Heaven was robbed, the entire town would've heard about it, so I assume Paul didn't pull it off. Maybe he tried to hire someone else to rob the salon, it didn't work out, and they killed him. Or maybe the buyer he lined up for the equipment killed him when Paul failed to deliver.

If Paul owes money to Jay Singh, maybe Jay killed him. That would be bad for Jay's business though, since dead people don't make debt repayments. But sometimes on TV, the loan shark kills the debtor as a warning to other debtors.

Maybe Kelly found out about the burglary plot, her husband's gambling habit, secret debt, or all of the above, and it pushed her over the edge, and she killed him.

Maybe Paul used the photos of Adam and Stephanie to blackmail the Murphys, and they killed him.

Or maybe Ryan is lying. If he is, it's an elaborate lie. There's one way to find out.

"Since I'm not scheduled to work this afternoon, I'm going to visit Jay Singh."

"That doesn't sound very safe, my dear. What if he is the killer?"

"I promise I'll only go if April comes with me." I make an X over my heart to assure Connie I mean it. "We won't go anywhere alone with him. At the very least, he might verify Ryan's alibi and eliminate him as a suspect."

Connie says nothing. She purses her lips and squints. The look on her face makes it clear that while she doesn't like my plan, she won't try to stop me.

"I have a book club meeting tonight, and Archie is a member, so I'll ask him if he remembers where Ryan was when Paul was murdered."

"Thank you," I say, smiling.

I pull out my phone and text April, asking if she's up for a road trip this afternoon. She is! We agree to meet after lunch and drive to Harmony Hills.

Eric texts me again, asking when we can meet. I holdback my reply until after April and I visit Jay. With any luck, I'll be able to give Eric a lead on a suspect that isn't Adam or me.

CHAPTER 12

I DROP off the online orders at the post office on my way home for a quick lunch before April and I visit Jay Singh. It's still cloudy and humid, but the drizzle has stopped for now. My curly hair expands in the damp air and, while I walk, I use the hair elastic on my wrist to secure it in a high ponytail.

Walking up to the house, it's weird to see Adam's car in the driveway on a weekday. Walking into the house, it's even weirder to see him sitting at the kitchen table on a weekday. He's focused on his new laptop, and I don't want to disturb him, so I walk into the kitchen unannounced.

"Hey!" He says without looking up.

"Hey. How's the new laptop?"

"I like it. I had to leave my old laptop with the firm when I resigned. It was company property.

Anyway, I'll need a laptop to start a law practice in Harmony Lake."

He looks at me and smiles.

"Oh, you aren't joining another firm?"

I assumed he would pursue a partnership elsewhere.

"No, it's time for a change," he replies. "I can't work anywhere for thirty days because of the thirty day non-compete clause I have with the firm, but on the thirty-first day, I intend to hang out my shingle and open for business. There aren't any lawyers in Harmony Lake, it's an underserved market. The closest lawyer is at least half an hour away in Harmony Hills, and I think he limits his practice to real estate law, if he's still there. He might've retired. I should look into that."

He picks up a pen and makes a note in the planner beside his laptop.

"How was your visit to the police station last night?" I ask. "I didn't hear you come in. Eric must've kept you pretty late."

He makes a sweeping gesture with his hand, "It was fine. I answered Eric's questions honestly and thoroughly. He kept my cell phone, so I went out this morning and bought this."

Adam holds up a shiny new cell phone and waves his empty hand with a flourish that would make Vanna White proud.

"It's two models newer than the old one. It's really advanced, and it can interact with Oscar!"

New technology is Adam's happy place.

"I already texted Hannah and gave her my new number."

"How did you explain it to her?" I ask, trying to mask my panic.

She knows Paul's death was murder, but I'm trying to avoid her finding out her parents are suspects.

"Relax," Adam says, "I told her I left the firm to open a practice in Harmony Lake. I explained that the laptop and phone belonged to the firm, and I had to leave them. She's fine with it."

He taps the screen of his new phone, then puts it down on the table. My phone dings; a text from a number I don't recognize.

"I assume this is you?" I ask.

"Yup." He nods. "Now you have my new number too."

I save his number to my phone and delete his old office and cell phone numbers.

"Adam."

"Mm hmm." He's staring at his laptop screen again.

"Adam. Look at me." I need to look in his eyes when I ask him what I'm about to ask him. We make eye contact. "Are you having an affair with Kelly Sinclair?"

His eyes open as wide as they can, and he raises his eyebrows so high, they almost disappear into his hairline.

"Of course not!" He insists. "Meg, why would you ask me that?"

"Then why are you communicating with her and meeting her?"

"Did Kelly mention this to you?" The shocked expression morphs into one of confusion.

"No," I reply. "Eric did. He asked me if I knew you and Kelly were communicating and if I knew about any meetings between you. I told him I know nothing, because I don't."

Adam hesitates. He's choosing his words carefully.

"It would be inappropriate for me to comment on any communication between myself and Kelly Sinclair."

His lawyer voice. This isn't Adam, my soon-to-be-ex-husband speaking, it's Adam the lawyer. I know this routine well.

"Is your relationship with Kelly protected by attorney-client privilege?" I ask.

He puts his right hand in front of him, palm toward the floor, and rotates his wrist. "It's complicated."

"Complicated because you have a personal relationship with her?" *C'mon, Adam, give me a clue.*

"No! Absolutely not!" he laments. "Stephanie is

the only personal relationship I've had, and it was a huge mistake, Meg. I've regretted it every day since it started–this summer, by the way. Long after you and I called it quits."

Not that long, but whatever.

"So Kelly isn't a client, and you don't have a personal relationship, but you can't give me a straight answer?" I clarify. "Is that what you're saying?"

"Kelly's not a client. She hasn't paid me for legal services, and I haven't represented her. Technically, we spoke as friends. I didn't even let her pay for my coffee, so I'm not violating attorney-client privilege if I tell you."

I sit across from him at the kitchen table, and he closes his laptop.

"Kelly texted me a couple of months ago and asked me to meet her for coffee. She asked me not to tell anyone, not even you. She insisted we meet away from Harmony Lake, and away from my office. We met at a coffee shop in the city. She told me Paul used to have a gambling problem and racked up significant debt. She said the gambling and the financial strain almost ended their marriage, but he got help for his addiction. They stayed together, and over time they paid off the debt. Now that they're back on their financial feet and the salon is doing well, Kelly worried what could happen if Paul gambled again. About her potential liability for gambling debts he might incur. She wanted advice on Paul-proofing her business and the building. We discussed various hypothetical options and scenarios for about an hour. After that, Kelly never contacted me again, but Paul did. A few days after Kelly and I met, Paul began texting me, demanding to know why I met with Kelly. He accused me of having an affair with her or trying to."

"What did you tell him? And did you tell Kelly that Paul contacted you?"

"I responded to one of Paul's texts and denied his accusation." Adam shrugs. "I told him I had no idea what he was talking about. He continued sending texts, and I ignored them. He left a couple of voicemail messages, and I ignored those too. I saved the messages, though, they're on the phone Eric kept. In one message, he said he knew Kelly and I were talking because he saw the text messages when he went through her phone, and he knew we met because he saw the entry in the calendar on her phone. I never told Kelly about it. She wasn't my client, and I didn't want to deal with Paul."

"Wow. Paul's control issues went beyond his role as town councilor to his role as husband." I get a glass of water and process what Adam just told me.

"Meg, I didn't kill Paul."

"I know."

"Have you given the police a statement yet?"

I'm not sure if Adam the lawyer is asking or Adam the soon-to-be-ex-husband.

"Kind of, I guess," I reply. "I answered questions that night, again yesterday morning at the store, and yesterday evening when Eric came to see you. And, he's been texting me today to meet again. He must be running out of things to ask me."

"You should have a lawyer present when he questions you. Let me give you a number..." He opens his laptop and starts tapping on the keyboard.

"I don't need a lawyer, Adam, it's fine. I haven't done anything wrong, and I have nothing to hide. I'd rather tell him everything I know and do whatever I can to help find the killer. I don't want to suspect everyone I know of murder. I want to eliminate us as suspects and get on with my life."

Did Paul make a habit of spying on Kelly? Why didn't he trust her? If she knew he was violating her privacy and checking up on her, would that make her angry enough to kill him?

Based on the conversation she had with Adam, it sounds like she knew, or at least suspected, Paul was gambling again.

CHAPTER 13

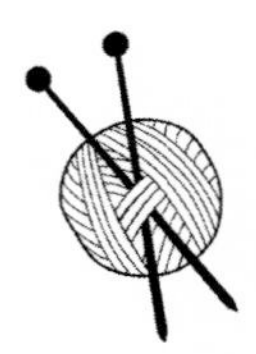

THANKS TO LIVING in the age of technology, a quick web search helped me find Jay Singh's address in Harmony Hills, and the GPS in April's car is helping us get there. It's raining, and we're on the highway almost halfway between Harmony Lake and Harmony Hills. Harmony Lake is on the south side of the Harmony Hills Mountains, nestled snugly between the mountains and the lake. Harmony Hills is on the north side of the Harmony Hills Mountains and is a suburb of the city located farther north. Harmony Hills is larger than Harmony Lake and doesn't have the same geographic restrictions, so it has a larger population and more amenities. Most residents of Harmony Lake make regular trips to Harmony Hills to visit the hospital, big box stores, various professionals, movie theatres, and everything else Harmony Hills has that our tiny town doesn't. The quickest route to get from Harmony Lake to Harmony Hills is a twenty to thirty-minute drive along the highway that runs through the mountains.

April and I agree it feels pushy showing up at a stranger's home unannounced, but I'm hoping the element of surprise will work to our advantage; Jay might not speak to us if he has time to think about it. And his reactions will be more candid than if he had time to prepare for our visit.

THE SINGH HOME IS A TWO-STOREY, two-car garage, red-brick house. It's in a newer subdivision with several speed bumps and no shortage of DRIVE SLOWLY: CHILDREN AT PLAY signs posted above the many NEIGHBOURHOOD WATCH signs. The front lawn and garden are meticulous, and the top of the driveway is littered with two tiny, training-wheeled bikes, hula hoops, a small basketball net, and remnants of chalk drawings washed away by the rain.

We pull up outside the house. It's not raining right now, but everything is wet. A thirty-ish year-old man wearing cargo shorts, a t-shirt and rain boots is jumping in puddles on the sidewalk with two small children. The kids wear identical bright green raincoats with frog eyes on the hoods and yellow rubber boots with toes painted like duck bills and eyes on the tops of the feet. They're freaking adorable!

"Ryan said Jay has twins. That's probably him," I say to April, whose eyes are also fixed on the two identical, adorable puddle jumpers.

"Awww, look at them!" she says. "Let's talk to him before our ovaries explode from the cuteness, or the neighbourhood watch wonders why we're sitting here."

We unbuckle our seat belts and April unplugs her phone from the car's console. We get out of the car and April locks it. The *beep* of the horn confirming it's locked gets the boys' attention. I smile and wave at them; they ignore me and jump in a puddle.

I introduce myself to Jay as a friend of Ryan's, and April introduces herself as a friend of mine. We shake hands and April and I gush over the cuteness of his sons. I tell Jay he has two of the cutest frog-duck puddle jumpers I've ever seen. He smiles at them with pride.

"If you're looking for a loan, there are online forms to fill out on the website, and I'll get back to you within twenty-four hours."

Jay Singh must be a modern, twenty-first century money lender.

"No. I'm not here for a loan, but since you

brought it up, I am super curious about your business. Is it a legitimate business? You have a website and everything?"

"Of course. Everything is above board. The service I provide is more common than you think."

He tells us he's a stay-at-home dad, and his sons just turned four. He and his wife, Jenna, were both nurses at Harmony Hills hospital, but after the twins arrived, finding an affordable daycare situation to accommodate their erratic shift schedules was impossible, so they decided Jay would stay home.

They had some money from an inheritance, and to replace Jay's income they were going to purchase one of the luxury condos in the new Harbourview Condominium development at the end of Water Street and rent it to tourists. But the development was a year from construction, and they couldn't wait. Jay did some research and realized that the return on investment would be higher and the risk more diversified if they made several high-interest, short-term loans.

I relate to their daycare struggle. I found out I was expecting Hannah within a few months of getting married, and about five years sooner than we'd planned. I had to leave school three semesters short of my degree when she was born. When Hannah started school full time, I was eager to finish my last three semesters and graduate, but I couldn't find a daycare solution that worked for all three of us. I was about to give up and accept that I'd have to wait to finish school, when Connie insisted that she and Colin, her husband, would love to help look after Hannah. They were like grandparents to her and spoiled her rotten. Colin passed away about five years ago, but Connie and Hannah still have a special bond.

"What I do is legal, though some people think it's unethical. Most of my clients are in Harmony Hills and Harmony Lake, and my job makes me privy to many secrets about many people."

Jay winks after that last sentence, and I get the sense he'd love to tell some of those secrets, but I already feel like, since Paul's death, I'm learning more about some of my neighbours than I care to know, so I interrupt him.

"That's why I'm here. I'd like to ask you some questions about a mutual acquaintance. Ryan tells me you know Paul Sinclair?"

"What about him? Does he owe you money?" Jay smirks.

Hearing him talk about Paul in the present tense makes me think he doesn't know about Paul's death, so I tell him someone murdered Paul on Tuesday.

"That's unfortunate. I guess I should expect a visit from the police soon," He says bluntly, sounding neither surprised by Paul's death, nor worried about a visit from the police.

"Ryan said when Paul tried to blackmail him, you helped him by giving him information to use against Paul. When Paul died, he was blackmailing my family, and I'm looking for information that might point the finger of suspicion away from us."

"He borrowed money from me," Jay offers. "I think he said it was to pay off some bad bets. He had trouble paying me back and fell behind with his scheduled repayments. He stopped returning my calls and emails, so my lawyer wrote a letter to Mr. and Mrs. Sinclair advising them I started the process of executing a writ of seizure on the building on Water Street."

I know about writs of seizure from Adam mentioning them. A writ of seizure gives Jay the right to force the Sinclairs to sell the building to repay the debt.

"But the business belongs to Kelly, not Paul," April interrupts. "Did they borrow the money together?"

"No, Paul borrowed the money alone. One reason people borrow from me, instead of a bank, and pay higher interest costs, is because they don't want their partner to know about the loan. His wife might own the business in her name alone, but they both own the building, so they're both notified. The letter and the threat are often enough to scare the debtor into finding my money."

"Was it enough to scare Paul?" I ask.

"Sure was. I heard from him the day he got the letter. It was sent by registered mail, and he's the one who signed for it, so I doubt his wife ever saw it. A few days later he asked to meet and paid the loan in full. With cash."

"Where did he get the cash so fast?" I think out loud, looking at April, not expecting a response.

"He said his brother-in-law lent it to him," Jay responds. "I don't know if it's true, and I don't care. People who need my services often have secrets they lie to protect. I take what they say with a grain of salt."

One twin asks if they can go in the backyard to dig for worms. Both boys are carrying a small bucket and shovel. So cute!

We follow the boys to the side of the house. April hangs back close to the sidewalk. She's being safe, so if something happens, she can get help. Jay opens the gate, and the boys run into the backyard. There's a large wooden play set with a slide, two swings, and a playhouse with a rock-climbing wall.

"That must be the play set Ryan assembled on Tuesday?" I ask, pointing to the large wooden structure.

"He assembled it, but, like, two weeks ago, not on Tuesday," Jay replies.

As soon as the words finish coming out of his mouth, his expression changes, and it's obvious Jay realizes that he just contradicted Ryan's alibi. "Actually, I can't remember for sure. Maybe Ryan was here on Tuesday night?" He furrows his brow, purses his lips, and directs his gaze down and to the right, trying hard to look like he's working out the correct date. Nice try, Jay. "Look, Ryan's a good guy," he asserts. "He's made a few mistakes and bad choices, but I consider him a friend. He must consider you a friend, too, if he told you about me and sent you here. There's no way Ryan killed Paul."

One twin offers his share of tonight's dessert if the other twin eats a worm. But only if he eats the whole worm.

Jay runs over to stop anyone from eating any portion of any worm. I yell after him, thanking him for his time, wishing him good luck with the worms, and telling him April and I will see ourselves out.

He waves to me in acknowledgement.

CHAPTER 14

"THAT WAS WORTH THE DRIVE!" I say as April navigates out of Jay's subdivision.

"I know, right! He said he has clients in Harmony Lake and is *privy to lots of secrets.* I wonder who else in Harmony Lake borrows money from him?"

"I'm not sure I want to know," I answer. "Life was easier forty-eight hours ago when the only secrets I knew were my own."

"And mine," April adds. "You know all my secrets."

"How can we find Paul's brother-in-law to ask him if he loaned Paul the money? If Ryan wasn't at Jay's house on Tuesday evening, where was he, and why would he lie?"

"I don't know the answers to those questions,"

April responds as she turns onto the main road that leads to the highway, "but I know that solving a murder in real life is harder than it looks on TV."

She's not wrong.

My phone dings: another attempt by Eric to arrange a meeting. I don't fancy being questioned at the police station, and I assume Adam will be home tonight. As luck would have it, Connie has a book club meeting this evening and Knitorious will be empty.

I reply to his text suggesting we meet at Knitorious after it closes. He confirms.

April puts on "No Scrubs" by TLC and turns it up loud. We sing at the top of our lungs as we merge onto the highway.

I GET to Knitorious twenty minutes before closing time and park behind the store.

Harlow is happy because my arrival coincides with his dinnertime. He corners me in the kitchenette and charms me until I feed him.

Connie is relieved I'm still alive, and the moneylender didn't kill April and me.

I fill her in about our visit with Jay Singh and remind her to please ask Archie about Ryan's whereabouts on Tuesday evening since Jay didn't confirm his alibi.

"He told you himself that he's not ethical, my dear. Maybe Ryan *was* there, and the money lender is mistaken or lying. But, of course, I'll ask. If the opportunity presents itself."

"He told me that some people believe his business is unethical, not that *he's* unethical," I correct her. "Also, you didn't see his reaction when he realized what he'd said."

I offer to close up so she can leave early, and tell her Eric is coming to the store to question me, but we'll leave before she gets home.

I haven't had dinner, and by the time Eric is due to arrive, I'm starving. Scrolling through the menu on the Ho Lee Chow website, I add items to the online cart until Eric knocks on the door.

I don't recognize him at first; he's not wearing a suit. He's wearing khaki, slim-fit trousers, a dark green, collared golf shirt, and brown leather slip-on shoes. The dark green shirt brings out the honey-coloured flecks in his eyes, and the short sleeves show off a pair of well-defined, muscular biceps and forearms. He's hot. I remind myself not to stare.

"Hi! Thanks for meeting me again," he says, standing aside, so I can lock the door after him.

He smells good, like a forest after it rains, and the sun comes out.

"No problem. You must be out of questions by

now. Or will I be answering the same questions I've already answered?"

I wonder if he's met with everyone else three times in two days, or just the top contenders on his suspect list.

"A bit of both." He smiles and puts a hand on his flat, probably-has-a-six-pack stomach.

Don't stare, Megan.

"Have you eaten? I'm starving and I thought I might order something to be delivered if that's OK."

"Great minds think alike, Eric."

I spin the laptop to show him the Ho Lee Chow menu I've been picking items from.

He adds a few items to the cart, and I submit our order. While we wait for dinner to arrive, I get dishes from the kitchenette. Harlow forces Eric to notice him by jumping onto the harvest table and pacing back and forth in front of him with his tail in the air while Eric strokes him and asks me about yarn.

What's the difference between a hank, a skein, a ball, and a cake? I explain that a hank is a loop of yarn that's loosely twisted, similar to the yarn that Kelly bought. A skein is yarn that's wound into an oblong ball. A ball is yarn that's wound into a round ball, and a cake is yarn that's wound into a cylindrical shape. To confuse him further, I explain that most people use *hank* and *skein* interchangeably. I gather yarn from the shelves as I explain to show him examples of each.

What does *ply* mean? Yarn consists of multiple strands twisted together: single ply is one strand of yarn, two-ply is two strands twisted together, three-ply is three strands twisted together, and so on. The yarn Kelly purchased was twelve-ply.

He also has questions about knitting needles: straight vs. circular, metal vs. wood, how to decide which size needle to use with which size yarn. At first, I assume his curiosity is because of Paul's murder, then I wonder if his interest is genuine. I'm sure it's related to the case, but I offer to teach him to knit, anyway. He declines, saying his job keeps him too busy for hobbies like knitting.

When he finishes testing my yarn and needle knowledge, we sit in the cozy sitting area and I pick up the hat I'm working on. I start the crown decreases while he asks me questions about my routine on Tuesday, and pets Harlow, who is curled up contentedly on his lap.

Our food arrives, and while we eat, he asks me about yesterday. I tell him, again, about Adam's visit to Knitorious to tell me Paul had copies of the photos and used them to blackmail us. Then I tell Eric he caught me off guard last night when he suggested Adam and Kelly were having an affair.

"I'm sorry how that played out, and I'm sorry I upset you," he says. "I didn't think there was anything between them, but I needed to be sure, and your reaction helped confirm my hunch."

I appreciate his apology, but don't respond because I still think it was a cruel way to confirm his hunch.

"Adam's affair with Mrs. Murphy must have upset you though..."

Eric likes to use unfinished sentences to ask questions. He starts a statement and lets his voice trail off at the end while he looks at you to finish the thought for him.

"Adam and I were married for almost 20 years. We met in university when I was 18, and by the time I was 20, we were married. I became pregnant soon after. We had a great marriage for a long time, but somewhere along the way, we grew apart. Our lives stopped revolving around each other and neither of us noticed. He focused on his career, I focused on being a Mum and being involved in the community. Next thing we knew, Hannah was the only thing we had in common."

I stop to drink some water.

"If you both decided it was over months ago, why are you still living under the same roof and keeping your separation a secret? Most divorced couples can't wait to get away from each other."

I want to ask him if he's speaking from experience, but I don't.

"This year was a big one for Hannah. She

finished high school and went away to university. We were determined that our separation wouldn't overshadow her last year of high school, so we decided Adam wouldn't move out until she left for university. The last thing she needed was everyone in town talking about our failed marriage and her broken home. Reputation is everything in a small town—especially in Harmony Lake. We're handling this transition like civilized, reasonable people. I've always put Hannah's interests above all else, and this divorce is no exception. We may not be a couple anymore, but we're Hannah's parents and we'll always be family. We're intent on coming out of this divorce as friends. Or at least friendly to each other. We'll see."

"No one in Harmony Lake knows you're separated?" Eric asks.

"The only people who know, other than Hannah, are April and Connie. Unless Adam confided in someone. I'm not angry or betrayed by his relationship with Stephanie Murphy. I haven't been in love with Adam for a long time. I want him to be happy and live a good life, I just wish he'd waited until he moved out, didn't send his girlfriend compromising photos, and maybe picked someone who wasn't already in a relationship."

Saying this out loud, to someone other than Connie or April, is cathartic. It's not easy pretending your marriage isn't broken. Living a lie is exhausting.

I wonder if Eric is married and is a dad. Has he ever disentangled his life from someone else's while causing as little damage as possible to his kids?

It's like playing catch with a hand grenade, except every time you throw it, you take one step backwards until you and the person you're playing catch with can't communicate anymore. So, you both just try to be slow, gentle, and intentional with each toss, grateful when the other person catches it, and it doesn't hit the ground, destroying your home, your lives, and your child.

We each choose a fortune cookie. Eric's says, "You are cleverly disguised as a responsible adult," and mine says, "Three people can keep a secret only if you get rid of two," which sounds ominous and creeps me out. I jokingly offer to trade fortunes with him, but he declines, saying he likes his non-creepy fortune better.

While clearing the dishes and throwing away the food packaging, I contemplate whether to tell Eric about my conversation with Ryan and the road trip April and I took to visit Jay. I want this case solved as fast as possible. The more information he has, the faster Eric can find the killer and clear the Martel name. I decide it's best to tell him.

If I'm lucky, maybe he'll tell me something in return that I don't already know about the case.

"I had an interesting conversation with Ryan Wright this morning."

I tell Eric about my conversation with Ryan, while watching him intently for a hint of a reaction. Nothing. Either this isn't new information, or Eric has an impressive poker face.

I double down and tell him about my conversation with Jay. Still no reaction.

When I finish talking, Eric gazes into the distance like he's thinking about something. Then he looks at me.

"I'm not from Harmony Lake," he states. "This is a small community, and the residents are... protective... of each other and information. They don't trust outsiders, and I'm an outsider. They're hesitant to open up to me."

He's choosing his words with intention. I live in this small, protective community, and he doesn't want to offend me. This is a pleasant change from last night. He's right, though. It takes a while for us to warm up to new people. We cater to tourists who visit Harmony Lake for a few days or weeks of the year. Some of them want the local experience, and we've learned to make them feel welcome and included while still protecting the heart of our community and keeping it just for us.

"I appreciate you sharing what you've found out with me," Eric continues, "but it's not a good idea for you to investigate and question witnesses.

Asking the wrong questions to the wrong people puts your safety at risk. But if people seek you out and share information with you, I'd appreciate you passing that information along to me."

I'm choosing to interpret this as a verbal disclaimer, like an ENTER AT YOUR OWN RISK sign at a construction site. It doesn't mean you *can't* enter the site; it just means if you do, you might get hurt, and it'll be your own fault because you ignored the sign. He didn't say no, he said it's not a good idea, and that isn't the same as no.

It would be easier for both of us, and less work for me, if he would say what he means, but I'm learning that Eric speaks in subtext. He answers questions without actually answering them, and now, it seems, he gives permission without actually giving permission. It must be a cop thing.

It's getting late, and I'm tired. I try to fight it, but a yawn escapes me, and I ask Eric if we're done with questions for the night. I turn off the lights and we say goodnight to Harlow. The cat follows us to the back door, then slinks upstairs to Connie's apartment. When we leave through the back door, Eric and I wish each other a good weekend, which makes me hopeful he won't question me again until at least Monday.

CHAPTER 15

FRIDAY, September 13th

Connie has yet another mystery appointment this morning. She doesn't tell me where she's going, which is unusual for her. I hope everything is OK and have to trust that she'll tell me if it isn't.

Friday and Saturday are our busiest days, so business is steady today. Harlow, planting his cuteness in a warm ray of sun in the front window for his morning nap, attracts a few passersby who come in to see him, making us appear busier.

Paul's murder is still the number one conversation topic around town. People want to know when the police will remove the crime scene tape. And when Kelly will come home.

I take advantage of the brief intervals between

serving customers to update the inventory on the website and finish Hannah's hat; I bind it off just before noon.

When Connie returns from her appointment, she brings me a sandwich from Deliclassy. It must be tuna because Harlow appears on the counter like a flash, showing serious interest in the bag.

"How was book club? It was pretty late when I left, but you still weren't back."

"It was fun! There was some confusion about what our September book is, so half of us showed up having read one book and half of us read another book. We solved it by breaking into two smaller groups, one for each book, and next month we'll switch!"

"I'm glad it worked out. Did you ask Archie about Ryan's alibi?"

"Yes, I did. Archie insists Ryan was with him. They watched the baseball game on TV and barbecued steaks. He says Ryan was with him from late afternoon until the next morning."

"I guess Ryan mixed up his Tuesdays, then. He must have been in Harmony Hills the previous Tuesday," I shrug.

"I've known Archie a long time, my dear. He wouldn't lie. I believe him."

"So do I," I say.

At least I think I do. I want to. Would Archie lie

to give his son an alibi? I think a lot of parents might tell a fib to protect their children.

Harlow and I eat our sandwich in the kitchenette, and the rest of the afternoon passes quickly.

We close the store and tidy up to prepare for tomorrow. Then I go home to have an awkward dinner with Adam. I can't remember the last time we had a meal alone. We struggle to find something to talk about aside from Paul's murder or Hannah.

As much as I enjoy a good small town murder mystery or true crime documentary, both feel a bit too close to home right now, so after dinner, I watch a stand-up comedy special, cast on the matching cowl for Hannah's hat, and knit until my eyelids feel heavy and I'm ready for bed.

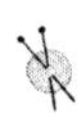

SATURDAY, September 14th

Saturday is our busiest day. Today is no exception. We're getting into the busy season. Knitters are embracing fall and planning their holiday knitting. As soon as the snow falls, we'll also be busy with tourists staying at the ski resorts. Saturdays will only get busier until after ski season.

After lunch, Connie's phone chimes. She reads the message, then hands me her phone. Customers are milling around the store, and she doesn't want to read it out loud.

It's a message in the WSBA group chat:

Libby: Paul's body was released to his family. His funeral is on Wednesday. A private service for family followed by a public celebration of life at the Irish Embassy. Details soon.

Libby is the owner of Latte Da, and the Irish Embassy is our local pub. The Embassy, as it's called by the locals, is owned by the O'Brien family. Sheamus manages the pub, and his parents, who are mostly retired, divide their time between Harmony Lake and Dublin, Ireland.

I hand Connie's phone back to her, and literally seconds later, a symphony of cell phone notifications chime throughout the store. Customers talk amongst themselves about Paul's arrangements. The speed at which news travels through Harmony Lake is astounding.

Tonight is trivia night at The Embassy. The knitting group that meets at the store each week has a team called Knitty By Nature. The winning team gets a free meal (lunch only) at the pub. Tamara meets us after the store closes, and we head over to The Embassy to win the free lunch! Tamara is a trivia buff and an occasional knitter, so we recruited her for our team. She's alone tonight because April took their fifteen-year-old son, Zach, to hockey practice. We don't win the free lunch, but thanks to Tamara, we're a close second.

Everyone in the pub speculates about Paul's murder, and harasses Sheamus for details about Paul's celebration of life, but Sheamus doesn't confirm or deny anything, and says he'll tell us more when he can.

SUNDAY, September 15th

This is the third Sunday since Hannah's left home, and so far, Sundays are when I miss her the most. It's the day we would do something fun together. On Sunday evenings we would have dinner as a family when Adam came home.

Since we can't be together as a family in person, we do the next best thing. Adam and I FaceTime Hannah together and have a virtual visit with her. She tells us about her classes, her new friends, and the fun, touristy things she's doing in Toronto.

We're careful not to mention Paul's murder, blackmail schemes, or police interrogations. When Hannah asks how Kelly is doing, I tell her that Kelly is staying with her sister. Adam quickly changes the subject.

Several times each day, I get the urge to text Kelly, ask how she's doing, and let her know everyone is thinking about her. But I don't want to impose. She has so much to deal with. As far as I know, she hasn't been back to Harmony Lake since Paul died. If she's not ready to deal with us, I won't force us on her.

I spend the rest of Sunday missing Hannah, cleaning the house around Adam while he works on his laptop, and giving the lawn and garden some much-needed attention.

CHAPTER 16

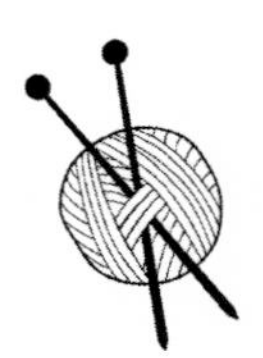

MONDAY, September 16th

Knitorious is closed on Mondays, so it's my day to drive to Harmony Hills to grocery shop and run errands I can't do in Harmony Lake.

I pull into the Shop'n'Save parking lot, turn the car off, and text April.

Me: I'm in HH today, do you need anything?

Whenever one of us comes to Harmony Hills, we text the other to see if they need anything. It's become a habit.

I push the button that opens the trunk and get out of the car to retrieve my reusable shopping bags. As I close the trunk, my phone vibrates in my pocket.

April: So am I! I was about to text you. Just about to go into Shop'n'Save.

Me: I'm in the parking lot, where are you?

April: Meet me at the door by the pharmacy.

I shove my phone in my pocket and head toward the pharmacy entrance where I find my friend.

"Why are you here on a Monday?" I ask mid hug. "You know I shop on Mondays. I would've picked up whatever you need."

"I know, but we have this... situation... called Zach. He's fifteen and eats *constantly.* We shop three times a week just to keep him fed. Also, they're having a ridiculous sale on butter this week, and T wants me to buy as many as I can carry. She's afraid they'll run out before the sale ends."

"If there's a limit on how many you can buy, I'll buy up to the limit, too, so T won't have butter anxiety," I offer.

We each get a cart and decide to start in the dairy section.

April puts the maximum amount of butter they allow each shopper to purchase at the sale price into her cart, and I do the same.

With our carts stacked with literally enough butter to supply a bakery, we meander up and down the aisles, picking up items and checking them off our lists as we go. We talk about our weekends, update each other on Hannah and Rachel, and strategize to get Tamara on Jeopardy, so she can win all the money, and she and April can retire.

We turn into the freezer aisle, and as April says she doubts Tamara would retire if she won on Jeopardy because she loves working at the bakery so much, Kelly Sinclair walks past the end of the aisle. She's with a woman I don't recognize. She's pushing a cart.

I tighten my grip on the handle of my butter-heavy cart and speed walk to the end of the aisle, trying to catch up to her. April speed walks after me.

"Where are we going? I need to get frozen pizza in this aisle."

"Kelly just walked by," I say.

I make a sharp left, speed walk past a display of peanut butter, then toilet paper, and look up the next aisle. No Kelly. I continue toward the next aisle, past a display of tomato sauce, then baby food. April breaks into a jog, and in a few strides, she and her butter-filled cart are beside me.

"Kelly Sinclair?" she asks.

"Yes. With a woman. They have a cart."

I look up the next aisle, no Kelly. April uses her impossibly long legs to outpace me and beats me to the next aisle. She looks up the aisle, then looks back at me and smiles.

"Found them!"

She turns her cart into the household cleaning

aisle. My cart and I follow her, and I think about how this would never happen in Harmony Lake; stores are too small for a foot chase. There are obvious benefits to small stores with short aisles.

Kelly is at the end of the aisle. Her hair is in a messy top knot, and she's wearing grey sweatpants, a matching grey hoodie, and white running shoes. She looks so different from the polished, glamourous Kelly I'm used to seeing in Harmony Lake that I'm surprised I recognize her. She's facing a shelf, comparing two items with one in each hand.

Her friend and I make eye contact. I don't recognize her. She's not from Harmony Lake. She says something to Kelly, then turns and walks away, disappearing as she turns at the end of the aisle.

When we're about halfway up the aisle, April calls her name.

Kelly turns to us, and her face lights up with recognition. April pulls her cart over to the side of the aisle, walks over to Kelly and gives her a hug. She says something in Kelly's ear and Kelly's red, swollen eyes become redder and fill with moisture.

I reach into my tote bag and grab my portable tissue holder. When April lets go of Kelly and steps back, it's my turn, and I give Kelly a long, tight squeeze. When we pull apart, I hold out the portable tissue holder for her to take, but she reaches into her purse on the top-level of her cart and pulls out her own portable tissue holder.

"I came prepared!" She attempts a laugh and dabs at her puffy, tired-looking eyes.

"Megan, I'm sorry I haven't been in touch. I meant to call and thank you for helping me the other night. Everything's been so busy since… I just haven't had time to call anyone."

"Please don't worry about it, Kelly," I assure her. "You're going through so much. No one expects you to do anything except take care of yourself. Nothing else matters."

"Everyone in Harmony Lake is thinking of you and hopes you're doing OK," April adds. "Do you need anything? You only have to ask," April chokes up at the end of her sentence.

Now we're all crying. It was only a matter of time.

"I'm fine. My sister,"—Kelly gestures to her left, where her friend, who I now assume is actually her sister, was standing before she walked away — "and brother-in-law are amazing. They fuss over me, and they've both missed work to help me out. My sister is here, she popped over to the pharmacy to fill a prescription. This week is so hard…" Kelly's voice hitches on the last word.

April and I each rub one of her arms while we fight to keep our own tears from streaming.

This would be a strange scene for someone

wandering up the aisle in search of dish soap; two emotional women with a bizarre amount of butter comforting a third, crying woman whose cart is... full to the brim with cleaning supplies? I try to hide my shock at the contents of Kelly's cart.

"What's with all the cleaning supplies, Kelly?" I ask quietly, trying not to sound critical or judgmental.

If purchasing excessive cleaning supplies is what Kelly needs to do to cope and get through this tragedy, we will support her.

"The police released the salon and the apartment," Kelly explains, "so I'm going over there when we're finished here. I plan to spend the rest of today and tomorrow deep cleaning."

She reaches for a box of rubber gloves on the shelf beside her and places them in her cart next to the box of rubber gloves already there.

"There's dust everywhere from fingerprinting and footprints from boots. Everything needs a thorough scrubbing."

"Do you need help?" I offer. "I'm a pretty thorough cleaner when I put my mind to it, and Knitorious is closed on Mondays, so I'm free."

"And after I deliver all this butter to the bakery, I can scrub too. The three of us could make quick work of it," April suggests.

"No, thank you, ladies. I want to do this on my own. I'm hoping it'll be cathartic. I plan to go home on Wednesday after Paul's service and open the salon as usual on Thursday."

"Well, you have my number if you change your mind."

I hope I don't sound relieved. I'm not prepared to go back there today. I'm not ready. The last place I want to go is where I found Paul's body. But I imagine it will be much worse for Kelly. She needs all the support she can get, so I'll suck it up if I have to.

Kelly invites April and I to attend Paul's celebration of life on Wednesday. We ask if we can bring anything or do anything to help, but she insists they've taken care of everything, and she wants people to focus on remembering Paul.

"He was such an amazing man. Everyone loved my Paul. My voicemail is full of people telling me how much they'll miss him and how generous and kind he was." She tears up and takes a moment to collect herself.

"Harmony Lake won't be the same without him," I say.

It's not a lie. Out of the corner of my eye, April glares at me.

"He was one of a kind," April adds.

It's my turn to glare at April.

"I should find my sister." Kelly puts both hands on the handle of her cart and prepares to move.

"Before you go…" I place a gentle hand on her

cart. "If the police released the building, does that mean they know who did it? Are they going to arrest someone?"

"They haven't said, but they don't tell me anything. This Sloane guy likes to ask questions, but he doesn't like to answer them."

"I've noticed," I sympathize.

Kelly's expression changes from sad to tense.

"I told Eric Sloane who did it," she exclaims. "I told him to arrest Ryan Wright, but he's still walking around Harmony Lake, a free man." She shrugs with both hands in front of her.

"How do you know it was Ryan?" April asks.

I'm glad April asked, because I want to know, but hesitated for fear of further upsetting Kelly.

Kelly looks at me. "Remember when I told you Paul didn't trust Ryan and didn't want him in the salon or apartment?"

I nod.

"Well, Ryan tried to talk my Paul into an insurance scam involving the business." She opens her eyes wide and pauses for a reaction. I open my eyes wide in response and make my best surprised face. "Ryan said he knows a guy who will pay big money for my new salon equipment. He told Paul it would look like a robbery. He said I could make an insurance claim to get the stolen equipment replaced. Ryan told Paul he would give us half of the proceeds."

"Wow!" I say out loud, despite intending to say it in my head.

"I know, right?" Kelly says. "I couldn't believe it. I thought Paul misunderstood him, but then he told me Ryan has done this kind of thing before. Apparently, he went to jail a few years ago for stealing from his employer and re-selling the stolen goods."

"What did Paul say when Ryan suggested this scheme?" April asks, shocked.

"He told Ryan we wanted nothing to do with it. He warned Ryan that if any of my equipment went missing, we'd go straight to the police and tell them it was Ryan who did it."

Paul has a pattern of lying and blackmail, and Ryan's history includes time in jail for a similar robbery scheme. Which one of them is lying, and which one is telling the truth?

Kelly and her cart of cleaning supplies make their way toward the pharmacy to find her sister, and April and I resume shopping and checking items off our lists.

"They don't look alike, do they?" April observes, gesturing to Kelly and her sister who are leaving the store with their purchases. "Kelly is blonde and lean, and her sister is brunette and curvy. Like you and me."

"She seems convinced Ryan killed Paul," I point out.

"She also seems convinced everyone loved Paul and thought he was a great guy," April counters. "It was like she was describing a different person. Grief must have a way of changing our perspective and making us remember only the best parts of the person we lost."

"Is her judgment clouded by grief, or is she blaming Ryan to keep the investigation focused on him and not on her?" I ponder aloud. We cash out and I follow April to her car to transfer the butter from my cart to her trunk. "Who has a stronger motive, Kelly or Ryan?" I ask.

"I think it's relative," April replies. "What isn't a big deal to one person might be enough for another person to commit murder."

"And they both gain from Paul's death," I add. "Kelly's business would be protected from Paul's gambling, and Ryan's criminal history would stay a secret."

"But did they both have opportunity?" April asks as she closes her trunk. "If Archie is telling the truth, Ryan couldn't have done it. Kelly had the opportunity. She was in the salon while Paul was upstairs. She just had to distract Mrs. Pearson and go up there and kill him."

After we say goodbye, I load my groceries into the trunk, and head home to take something for the headache I feel coming on.

CHAPTER 17

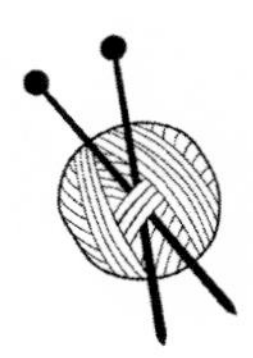

Wednesday, September 18th

I'm walking along Water Street en route to Knitorious to meet Connie. We're going to the Irish Embassy together for Paul's celebration of life.

The warm, sunny day is a stark contrast to the sombre, serious mood of the town. It's not everyday Harmony Lake buries one of its own. Never mind someone as young as Paul or a murder victim.

The WSBA and the town council decided Water Street businesses could close early today so everyone can attend Paul's celebration of life. The irony of Water Street closing early isn't lost on me. Paul devoted his life to enforcing compliance with every town and WSBA bylaw and ordinance. I doubt he would approve of closing early on a business day for anyone's funeral, even his own.

But maybe the point is to honour Paul in a way that would mean something to him by changing the rules to accommodate him. Or maybe it's a passive-aggressive way to violate a bunch of bylaws at once, since there's nothing Paul can do about it.

What to wear was a tough decision. The weather is too fall-like for a summer dress, but too warm for a winter dress. I settled on a knee-length, black jersey-knit dress with three-quarter length sleeves, and black calf-high leather boots. I pulled my hair into a French twist and chose not to fight with the few rebellious curls around my face that refused to cooperate. To add a bit of colour to my all-black ensemble, I switched out my black tote bag for my pumpkin-coloured tote bag. I always carry a tote bag large enough to accommodate my usual purse items, along with a knitting project or two. Over the years, I've acquired an impressive bag collection.

Adam texted to say he'll be late due to an appointment. I overheard him on the phone yesterday, and it sounded like he was planning to view an apartment. I hope he likes it, wants to live there, and will move out any day now.

We agreed to tell friends and neighbours about our separation. After today, so we don't upstage Paul's day. Today, we'll attend Paul's celebration of life together to keep up appearances. We're quite good at faking it, we've had lots of practice.

Arriving separately won't raise any eyebrows because the entire town knows Adam is a workaholic, and everyone is used to me arriving at events on my own.

I'm about to reach into my bag for my keys, but I decide to turn the handle and see if the door is already unlocked. It is. I open the door to Knitorious and listen for the jingle. The familiarity makes me feel warm and comfortable. Connie is in the cozy area with Archie Wright and two ladies from the book club.

"Hello, my dear!" Connie waves me over. "We're just having a quick cup of tea before we head over. We thought we'd arrive as a group, apparently several community groups are sending a delegation, so we decided we would too!"

Harlow is curled in a ball and sleeping on her lap.

I greet Connie's friends and make polite small talk while I help clear the teacups from the large square coffee table.

Our envoy leaves Knitorious, and we walk up Water Street to the crosswalk in front of The Irish Embassy. There are a few people dressed in dark, conservative attire loitering outside the pub entrance. They're chatting and soaking up the pleasant weather.

Archie opens the pub door and holds it while the rest of us file past him. The pub is packed. One step inside and we hit a wall of darkly clad people crammed too close together. Personal space does not exist here, we're literally rubbing shoulders with each other. Being on the shorter side, I rub just below the shoulder of most people.

I'm used to standing room only during tourist season, but it's never been as busy as this wake.

The Irish Embassy is a good-sized pub. It's the equivalent of two stores. The main floor has a long, double-sided bar in the centre with stools lining both sides of the bar. The bar is surrounded by various seating, booths along the walls, tables and chairs in the centre, and a couple of cozy sitting areas with sofas and club chairs around a fireplace.

There's a centre hall staircase behind the bar that leads upstairs where two large function rooms and Sheamus' office are located. There's a large open foyer overlooking the main floor with an intricate wood railing to lean on. Upstairs is closed to the public and available only for private functions. Behind the staircase there's more seating and the patio doors.

"Wow!" I say as I turn to look at Connie.

"He was young and involved in every committee and group in town." She shrugs. "I expected a full house, but I never imagined this!"

We suck in our shoulders and try to make ourselves as small as possible as we move through the crowd.

Lucky for me, April is tall and easy to spot. Her blonde head is about ten feet ahead.

"Excuse me! Pardon me! Sorry! Can I just squeeze past? Thank you!" I repeat as I navigate through the packed space. I regret my tote bag because of the extra space it takes up, and I'm envious of April who never carries a purse, just a wristlet that acts as both a wallet and phone case.

"I made it!" I declare triumphantly, then give April and Tamara a hug. "But I lost Connie along the way."

I scan the surrounding area, but there's no sign of Connie. The crowd absorbed her.

We discuss how warm it is with so many people so close together when Tamara points out the top of Adam's head, weaving its way through the crowd in our direction. I squeeze closer to April to make room for him.

Adam greets April and Tamara with a hug and cheek kiss. Watching them chat, I can't help but notice how flattering Adam's tailored suit is. He's always been handsome, but age and maturity have increased his attractiveness.

My mother said a well-tailored suit is to women what lingerie is to men. She was right. I catch myself giving him an appreciative head-to-toe-glance and feel a twinge of sadness remembering how once upon a time, seeing Adam dressed up and watching him charm a room would elicit a stronger physical response from me than just an admiring glance. I can't remember the last time my heart skipped a beat, or I felt the flutter of butterflies in my belly with Adam.

I'm trying to figure out the moment everything changed, and we stopped being in love, when the person standing behind me bumps me. We turn and apologize at the same time.

"Hi Phillip. Sorry to bump into you. Sometimes the force of the crowd just kind of moves me, you know?"

Phillip Wilde is my neighbour at home and at work. I smile and place a hand on his shoulder, steadying myself against the movement of the crowd. He leans in and we exchange a double cheek kiss.

"I know what you mean," he whispers in my ear because that's how close he is. "It took us twenty minutes to make our way over to Kelly to give our condolences. I don't think I'll last much longer in this suit. It's too warm in here."

He fans his hand in front of his glistening face.

"I hear ya!" I sympathize with him about the crowd. Being on the shorter side, crowds overwhelm me. I feel invisible when I'm surrounded by many people, like I'm being swallowed up. Suddenly, the atmosphere changes and the crowd loosens up. We can spread out a bit, move our elbows, and breathe deeper. I stand on my tippy toes to look around the pub. "Where is Kelly?" I ask.

Phillip points over his left shoulder, raises his eyebrows and says, "About twenty minutes that way. She's with her sister- and brother-in-law near the fireplace. You might get there in ten minutes since the crowd has eased up. And if you don't run into too many people."

"In this town?" I joke. "Where everyone knows everyone else?"

We laugh and I turn back to Adam, April, and Tamara.

"Sheamus opened the patio door and upstairs," Adam says, looking up and pointing toward the ceiling.

Grateful for the extra space, I silently thank Sheamus for relieving the pressure and letting in fresh air. I look where Adam is pointing and watch people spill into the open area at the top of the stairs. My gaze follows the wooden railing until it lands on Eric. He's leaning against the railing, drink in hand, scanning the crowd below. When our eyes meet, I smile and wave. He smiles back and lifts his drink.

Interesting. I guess it makes sense he would be here, watching and listening. Does this mean he thinks the killer is here? Blending in with everyone else, pretending to be a grieving friend and neighbour? I shudder and pull myself back to the here and now.

"We should find Kelly," I suggest. "Phillip said she's with her sister and brother-in-law near the fireplace." I jerk my head in the direction Phillip pointed to earlier.

We move single file through the less crowded room, stopping every few feet to say hello to a neighbour, or hug a friend.

When we get to Kelly, there's a line of people ahead of us waiting to offer their condolences. Even grieving and traumatized, she's beautiful and elegant. Her blonde hair is styled in a low chignon, and she's wearing a thin, black, long sleeve turtleneck, a pair of high-waisted, black, wide-leg trousers, and simple black pumps. Her wedding ring and gold stud earrings are her only jewelry. She's not wearing any makeup and her swollen eyes are red from crying, and probably from lack of sleep. She looks exhausted. Poor Kelly. She's having the worst week of her life, but she still puts on a smile and deals with a town's worth of people vying for a few minutes with her.

My heart breaks for her, and I feel like a huge jerk. She's devastated by her husband's death, and here I am wondering if she could be his killer.

Kelly handles everything around her with grace and poise. As I admire her strength under such stress, a man's hand comes into view. It disappears behind Kelly's upper back, and his arm moves up and down in a rubbing motion. I follow the arm to see the rest of the man attached to it.

It's Fred!

Why is Fred Murphy is rubbing Kelly's back?

CHAPTER 18

I LOOK AWAY from Fred just long enough to grab April's arm.

"Are you seeing this?!" My attempt to whisper sounds more like an angry hiss.

April's eyes widen when she sees Fred.

"Is that?" April asks, incredulous.

"Yup! Fred the blackmailer," I seethe before she finishes her sentence. "Why is he standing with Kelly?"

I should stop trying to whisper. Subtlety doesn't seem to be an option for me right now.

"If that's Fred"—April points to Fred—"is the woman on the other side of Kelly his wife, Stephanie?" She points to the woman. "Are Stephanie Murphy and Kelly sisters?" she asks with a puzzled expression.

April faces Fred, but looks at me when she speaks, "I'm sure she's the same woman who was with Kelly at the Shop'n'Save. Remember?"

Whoa! This realization blows my mind.

I scan the room for Adam. He's near the bar chatting with Sheamus. Narrowing my eyes on my target, I suck in my breath and march over there.

"Hi Sheamus." I smile at him and clench Adam's forearm, "You have your hands full today. It's a full house. Do you mind if I borrow Adam?"

Without waiting for a response, I lead Adam to a less-populated corner of the pub. I look him in the eye.

"Is that your girlfriend standing next to Kelly Sinclair? Look behind me, eleven o'clock."

Adam looks. He blinks and does a double take. His reaction is response enough; the woman beside Kelly is Stephanie Murphy. Stephanie and Kelly are sisters. Fred Murphy was Paul's brother-in-law.

Overwhelmed as I connect the mental dots, I find the nearest table and sit down. It's already occupied, but there's an empty chair. I smile at the people already sitting there.

"Do you mind if I just sit for a moment and catch my breath?"

"Of course," they respond out of sync, smiling politely. One of them asks me if I need anything. "Just to rest for a moment, thank you," I force a smile.

I fiddle with my ring and observe Stephanie from the safety of the full table. Stephanie and Kelly aren't at all alike, and I don't just mean their appearance.

Where Kelly is blonde, slender, and graceful, Stephanie is brunette, curvy, and seems uncomfortable greeting people and making small talk. The word *mousy* comes to mind. Kelly has beautiful taste and a classic sense of style, Stephanie's grey pant suit is a size larger than her body, and her cream-coloured blouse and sensible cream flats are, without a doubt, function over fashion.

I bear a closer resemblance to Stephanie than Kelly does. We're the same height, both have curly brown hair, fair skin, and a similar body type—a good helping of boobs and hips with a small waist. The similarities are a bit creepy. Maybe Adam has a type. It would make more sense to me if he chose someone who bore no resemblance to me.

"I swear, I had no idea they were sisters." Adam appears next to me. I get up, thank the other table occupants, and walk away. Adam follows me, continuing to speak. "Honestly, Meg, I didn't know Stephanie was married until Fred blackmailed me, never mind knowing anything about her extended family."

He sounds sincere. Gob smacked, I say nothing in response and purse my mouth into a thin line.

"She doesn't wear a ring," Adam continues. "She never talked about her family, and she didn't have any photos or personal items in her office. I knew about her cat. She talked about the cat and showed me photos of him on her phone. She never mentioned a husband. But now it makes sense why Kelly didn't want to meet for coffee near my office."

I glance at Stephanie's ring finger. He's telling the truth; she isn't wearing a ring. In fact, she isn't wearing any jewelry at all.

Maybe Stephanie didn't have any family photos in her office, but Adam did. Lots of them. The most recent addition to his collection was a photo of the three of us at Hannah's graduation ceremony.

When Stephanie and I made eye contact at Shop'n'Save on Monday, she must have recognized me from the photos in his office. That would explain why she disappeared to the pharmacy.

"She knew she was married, and you both knew you were married, even if it is in name only," I remind him. "You also knew that you were a senior partner, and she was a junior associate. The relationship was against company policy. Not to mention unethical. It put your livelihood and our family at risk," I admonish.

Maybe next time, he'll ask a few questions before he gets in bed with someone and sends them compromising photos.

We stand in silence. While I compose myself, he

recovers from the shock of his wife and girlfriend being in the same room at the same time.

"We should say hello to Kelly and give our condolences," I finally say as I turn and walk toward the condolence line.

April and Tamara go first. I watch as April introduces herself to Fred as though they've never met before and shakes his hand. Well played, April.

Watching them shake hands reminds me I need to pick up more of those portable hand sanitizer bottles for my purse and car; it's almost cold and flu season. I'm about to reach into my bag and rummage around for a bottle, so I can use it before and after I shake Fred and Stephanie's hands, but Tamara moves on to talk to Kelly, and it's my turn to greet Fred.

Following April's lead, I shake his hand, fake-introduce myself as Kelly's friend, and tell him I'm sorry for his family's loss. He fake-introduces himself as Fred, Paul and Kelly's brother-in-law, and thanks me for coming. I tell him Kelly mentioned how supportive he and his wife have been, while silently hoping he feels as awkward as I do with all this pretending.

Tamara moves along to Stephanie, and I move along to Kelly. I wipe the hand that touched Fred on my dress to banish the disgust I feel after touching the blackmailer.

While Kelly and I hug, I tell her to call, text, or

show up anytime day or night if she needs anything. I tell her the town already feels different without Paul. It's not a lie.

I move along to Stephanie and extend my hand. Her handshake is limp. When she tries to end the handshake, I tighten my grip just enough to prevent her from pulling her hand away. Then I place my other hand over our conjoined hands.

"I've heard *so much* about you." I let Stephanie pull her hand away from mine. She looks uncomfortable. Good. Though I get the sense she's generally uncomfortable. Blackmailing witch. "Kelly says you've been amazing this week. She's so lucky to have you. She says you and Fred took time away from work to support her. What do you do again?"

I maintain eye contact, and when she averts her eyes, I move my head to compel her to look me in the eye again, engaging her in some kind of weird, passive-aggressive staring contest. I'm determined to win. I don't even blink.

"I'm an attorney," she replies, her voice squeaky and mouselike.

"Right! I remember now," I say, still maintaining eye contact. I force a fake smile and summon my most chipper voice. "I believe you know my husband, Adam Martel." I turn to Adam as he finishes his conversation with Kelly. "Adam, you know Stephanie, right? You work together, I think?"

I look back at Stephanie. "I'm sorry, I meant to say *worked.* Adam resigned last week, but I'm sure you know all about that." I watch her squirm, then continue. "Such a small world! Stephanie, we're so sorry for your family's loss," I say, tilting my head and mustering a consoling tone of voice so sarcastic it sounds sincere.

I walk away, watching Adam and Stephanie's interaction. I don't see any sparks or chemistry between them. If there's still any attraction, it's not palpable. In fact, they look downright awkward, but that might be because of the scene I made. They shake hands, and he walks away. I hope their exchange was as uncomfortable as it looked.

"What was that, Meg?" Adam asks.

"I'm sorry," I respond. "I've never met my husband's girlfriend before. I don't know what etiquette is in this situation. *Please forgive me*." My words drip with disdain.

I look away from him because I'm fighting the urge to yell and say things I'll regret. I gravitate to April and Tamara.

"Stop calling her my girlfriend. She's not my girlfriend," Adam asserts, rolling his eyes, which only makes me more frustrated.

"Mistress? Concubine? Significant other? What label do you two prefer?" I ask. "Is it awkward having your wife and *girlfriend* in the same room?"

"I'm going to the bar to get a drink and give you

some space. I'll get you a drink too. You need one," he says calmly.

He turns to April and Tamara, "Ladies, can I get you anything from the bar?"

While avoiding looking at Adam, I notice an elderly couple approach Kelly with a plate of food and motion for her to sit by the fireplace.

The woman puts the plate down in front of Kelly and cuts the food into bite-size pieces. Recognizing a fellow mum when I see one, I deduce that the elderly couple is Kelly's parents.

The family settles in the sitting area by the fireplace. Then Fred leans over to Stephanie, says something in her ear, and she nods. Fred gets up, slips away from his in-laws, and strides toward the door. I'm right behind him.

CHAPTER 19

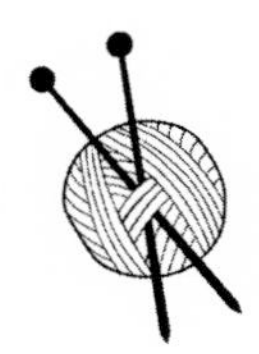

ADAM and I make eye contact as I follow Fred past the bar. I mouth, "Stay here," exaggerating each word so Adam can read my lips.

I follow Fred onto the sidewalk in front of the pub. He turns the corner and disappears in the alley beside the building. So that's what I do too.

Fred's upper body and left foot rest against the brick wall. His head lowered, his left hand cupping a lighter he's flicking in his right hand. There's a cigarette between his lips.

"Filthy habit," I say to announce my presence.

He looks at me, pulls a pack of cigarettes from his shirt pocket and extends his arm toward me, offering me one. I raise my hand in a stop gesture and shake my head no. I take a step closer, but make sure I'm visible from the sidewalk, so if I scream someone can find me.

"So, you're Paul's brother-in-law. I didn't see that coming."

Fred exhales a cloud of smoke.

"I assumed you knew," he says, "Doesn't everyone in this town know everything about everyone?"

I used to think so, but the past seven days have taught me there are a lot of secrets in Harmony Lake, and I'm happier not knowing most of them.

"Well, you don't live in this town. I'd never seen you before you showed up to blackmail us. I saw you arguing with Paul the day he died, and I mentioned it to the police. Why did you give Paul the photos? So, he could blackmail us too?"

"I didn't blackmail you. I blackmailed Adam," Fred clarifies.

He takes a long drag from his cigarette.

"Same thing," I point out.

"I didn't give Paul the pictures. We didn't know how he got them until after he died. Steph texted Kelly and told her about the affair the day before Paul died and sent the pictures to her. Kelly told the police she thinks Paul found the pictures when he was nosing around her phone. He stole them. Steph didn't tell Kelly who she was having an affair with. She only said it was a guy from work," He chuckles. "You should've seen her face when she found out he was your husband."

Fred chuckles again and slaps his knee, then looks at me without turning his head towards me.

How did Paul know Adam was Stephanie's affair partner? He could have recognized Adam's tattoo, but I'm not sure Paul ever saw it. More likely, he knew Adam and Stephanie worked together and took a stab in the dark that it was Adam. Then, Adam unknowingly confirmed Paul's suspicion by not denying it when Paul blackmailed us.

"I would never give the pictures to Paul. He's sneaky, and he'd use them for his benefit." Fred flicks ash from the tip of his cigarette. "I don't want the world to know my wife slept with your husband. If Paul knew, that's what would have happened. The entire world would know. At least now that he's dead, I don't have to deal with him or his problems anymore."

He takes another long drag from what's left of the cigarette.

"What did you and Paul argue about in the car?" I ask.

I have nothing to lose by asking. This could be my only chance to question Fred, so I'm asking all my questions now, while he's talkative.

"Paul owes me money. He told me he would pay me back by blackmailing Adam with the pictures. I was angry that he had the pictures. I wanted him to delete them and pretend he never saw them. But Paul's greedy, and there's no way he'd delete them if he could use them to squeeze money out of someone."

Fred says all of this matter-of-factly, like he has nothing to hide. He flicks the cigarette butt into the distance, and we watch it disappear.

Paul told Jay his brother-in-law loaned him the money to repay his debt; Fred just confirmed that Paul owed him money.

"If Paul owed you money, why kill him? He can't pay you back if he's dead."

I take a big step backwards in case Fred freaks out about being accused of murder, and I need to run.

"I didn't kill Paul. But he tempted me more than once, trust me," he answers, shaking his head. "I was asleep when Kelly called from the police station to tell us what happened. I was so tired from the previous two days. After learning about Steph's affair, talking with her to save our marriage, dealing with you and Adam, and arguing with Paul, I was so exhausted, I passed out after dinner and slept like I was in a coma. Steph had a hard time waking me up to go to the police station. She had to drive because I kept nodding off and couldn't stay awake."

He uses his left foot to push himself away from

the wall and stands with both feet on the ground, facing me.

"Look, I don't like Paul and I don't trust Paul, but Kelly loves him, and I love her like a sister. I love my wife, and it hurts her when Kelly suffers, so I would never do that to them. Anyway, I never expected Paul to pay me back. Before he died, he was spiralling financially." He twirls his index finger down in a circular motion. "Even dead, he's still costing me money."

Fred chuckles and coughs a phlegmy smoker's cough.

"How is your dead brother-in-law costing you money?" I ask.

"Who do you think paid for all this?" he answers my question with a question and gestures vaguely around us. "Kelly can't afford this spread. She also can't cover the cost of the funeral or cremation. Steph and I are footing the bill. When I heard he died, I thought at least his life insurance would cover his final expenses, but we found out yesterday he let the premiums lapse almost a year ago. Aside from the business, Kelly has nothing."

With that, Fred walks past me, rounds the corner, and returns to the pub.

I follow him around the corner and lean against the wall near the pub door, taking a moment to process my conversation with Fred.

Instead of eliminating suspects, I'm uncovering

more reasons to keep them on the list. First, Ryan, with his robbery scheme, criminal history, and revolving door of alibis. Next, Kelly, who wants to protect her home and business from her husband's financially destructive behaviour and stop him from snooping through her phone. Then there's Fred, who admits he hated Paul, admits he was angry when Paul threatened to expose Stephanie and Adam's affair, and was tired of giving Paul money.

As much as I hate to admit it and find it impossible to believe, I have to admit that Adam belongs on the suspect list too. Paul blackmailed him, and Adam didn't come home the night Paul was killed. He'd already lost his job because of the affair and maybe being blackmailed on top of everything else was too much to bear and pushed Adam over the edge.

Adam is just inside the pub door on the left, and Eric is on the right. I don't acknowledge Eric because I'm angry at him; he knew Kelly and Stephanie were sisters and didn't tell me. He stood back and let me get blindsided. Again. It's like watching me squirm is his hobby, or something.

I accept the glass of Pinot Adam offers me and take a long sip.

"Are you OK?" Adam asks. "I worried when he came back in and you didn't. I was about to look for you."

"I'm more confused than before I spoke to him, but other than that I'm fine," I mumble.

I take a deep breath and repeat, *heavy shoulders, long arms,* a few times in my head to help release the tension in my neck and shoulders.

Out of the corner of my eye, flailing arms get my attention. It's April. With the crowd thinning out, she, Tamara, and Connie found a booth.

Adam and I join them. I sit down, put my tote on the floor under the booth and fill them in on my conversation with Fred.

April and I are both in awe of Kelly's lying skills. At the grocery store, she didn't let on that she knew about Stephanie and Adam. Also, neither of us recall her referring to her sister by name, just as "my sister," and now I wonder if that was intentional. But Kelly invited me to Paul's celebration of life today, so she knew I'd find out her sister and Stephanie Murphy are the same person. Maybe I'm over thinking it. Kelly is so deeply mired in her own grief that lying to me or covering for her sister's poor decisions isn't on her radar right now.

"Well, either she's grieving and doesn't care, or she's an academy award worthy actor," Connie observes.

"Paul spied on Kelly's phone? Maybe she found out and got angry. Or maybe she found out he blackmailed Adam and threatened to expose her sister, and it made her snap," Tamara surmises.

It seems like there were trust issues in Paul and Kelly's marriage, at least on Paul's side. Paul's reaction when he found out Kelly texted and met with Adam in the summer is proof of that. I'm careful not to share this bit of information because Adam told me in confidence. Aside from me, the only person he told is Eric Sloane. If only Adam was as discreet with his personal relationships as he is with his professional ones, we wouldn't be caught up in this tangled yarn of a murder investigation.

"Until today, I thought Fred was the least likely suspect because Paul owed him money, and it's hard to collect a debt from a dead man. But Fred said he didn't expect Paul to pay him back. Also, the family thought Paul had insurance, but yesterday they found out he stopped paying the premiums almost a year ago. So, maybe Fred killed Paul for the insurance and it backfired," I suggest.

"I think Fred is the strongest contender for the title of Killer," April says. "If we were betting, I'd put my money on him."

"I don't know," I say.

I bite the inside of my lip while I wrestle with the gut feeling that Fred didn't do it.

"He kept referring to Paul in the present tense, you know? Like he said, 'I *don't* like Paul. Paul *owes* me money. He *is* sneaky.' Wouldn't the killer use past tense? And he didn't hesitate to talk to me. He acts like he has nothing to hide."

Maybe he's fed up with being a murder suspect and wants to wrap this up already. If that's the case, I relate because I feel the same way.

"We know he's capable of blackmail, and lying, so how big of a leap is murder?" Connie theorizes.

Everyone shrugs and nods their heads. I'm conflicted. Logically, I know Fred is a strong suspect, but my instincts don't agree.

"Are you ready to head out?" Adam asks me.

"I think I'll stay and have another glass of wine. Then I'll walk Connie home. I'll see you at home," I reply, smiling.

"Meg, there's a murderer in our midst, and you're asking questions and trying to figure out who it is. You could be in danger. I'll feel better if I walk you and Connie home."

He lays out his argument using his lawyer voice, and I hate it when he uses his lawyer voice with me.

"I'll be fine, Adam," I insist brusquely. "You can leave. I'll text you when I leave. You don't have to worry."

"Archie and some members of the book club are coming to Knitorious for tea after this, so I won't be alone anyway, but thank you, Adam." Connie reaches over and squeezes his hand.

"I'll keep Megan safe," Eric offers, suddenly standing beside our booth. Where did he come from? He looks at me. "Megan, I'd like to speak with you before you leave. Then I'll see you home safely. If that's all right with you, of course."

"It's fine," I say. I look at Adam. "I'll see you at home."

Adam says goodbye to the table, thanks Eric, and leaves.

"I'll be sitting by the bar whenever you're ready," Eric says before he walks away.

"Megan? Why are you *Megan* and T and I are *Ms. Shaw* and *Ms. Shaw*?"

"Dunno." I shrug. "He told me to call him Eric, so I told him to call me Megan."

"I need to figure out who killed Paul so I can get on with my life," I say.

Connie places her hand on top of mine and gives it a gentle squeeze.

"I'm going to get us another round of drinks. Or two!" April announces.

CHAPTER 20

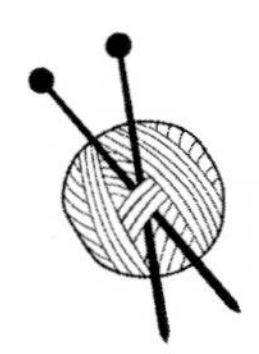

WITH A SLIGHT BUZZ from three glasses of wine on an empty stomach, I wander over to the bar. I find Eric perched on a bar stool with a plate of wings and a drink in front of him. I assume the drink is non-alcoholic because on TV police officers never drink while on duty.

"Is that from the local microbrewery?" I point to his pint glass.

"Only if the local microbrewery brews ginger ale," he replies, smiling. "Wing?"

He nudges a plate of wings toward me. Shaking my head, I raise my hand to say no thank you and climb onto the stool next to him at the almost-empty bar.

"I can't believe how busy it was in here earlier.

I've never seen so many people crammed into The Embassy," I say, making small talk.

"It was crazy," he agrees. "It was difficult to observe everyone. But I observed you racing out of here after Fred. How did that go?"

He gets right to the point. All business, this guy.

"I'm sure he didn't tell me anything that you don't already know. Like how you knew Stephanie and Kelly are sisters, and I didn't."

It's a relief to get this off my chest. One thing I've learned this week is to speak up when I'm upset and not shove my feelings aside. It's not my job to spare other people from having uncomfortable feelings at the expense of my own. I deserve to be heard too. Everybody does. As of today, I promise myself I will say how I feel and not ignore my feelings for the sake of not rocking the boat. And I will keep this promise at least until this wine buzz wears off.

"Until I saw the look on your face, I didn't know you weren't aware of the relationships. Harmony Lake is a small town, everyone seems to know everyone else, so I assumed you knew. I'm sorry that was awkward for you, it wasn't my intention."

Maybe he didn't blindside me on purpose.

"Thank you," I reply. "Why were you watching me?"

Was a cop assigned to watch every suspect?

"I wasn't watching *you*," he clarifies. "I was

watching the condolence line. It was busy in here, and I had to narrow my focus, so I monitored the condolence line from upstairs while a few non-uniforms wandered the crowd with their eyes and ears open."

While Eric finishes his wings and ginger ale, I fill him in on my conversation with Fred and share the conclusions that Connie, April, Tamara, and I came to earlier.

"I appreciate the information, it's more helpful than you realize, but Adam is right to be concerned about your safety. There's a murderer in this town, and they might know you're asking questions and talking to me. If they think you're getting too close, you could be in danger. You need to stop investigating and get on with your life."

His concern seems sincere, and not an excuse to convince me to get my nose out of his case, though I'm sure that's part of it.

"I need you to solve this murder because Adam and I are suspects. We have a daughter. I don't want her to think her father had an affair with a married woman, someone blackmailed us because of it, and one of us killed the blackmailer. Part of it being true is bad enough. It will be easier to explain to her when someone else is behind bars for Paul's murder," I explain. "Adam is a lawyer. Being a suspect in a murder investigation could destroy his career. I mean, would you hire a lawyer who may have killed the person who was blackmailing him? The affair already cost him his partnership at the firm."

I choke up, and my cheeks flush with angry heat. Talking about how this could affect Hannah makes it too real. I take a deep breath, dab my eyes with a napkin from the bar and compose myself.

"If I tell you something, do you promise not to tell anyone?" Eric asks just above a whisper.

He makes a fist and extends his pinky finger for a pinky swear. I hook my pinky finger around his.

"Promise." I use my other hand to make an X over my heart, so he knows I mean it. "I pinky swear, *and* I cross my heart and hope to die, so spill."

"We've eliminated Adam as a suspect. Security video footage and his keycard for the office building verify that he arrived at work early in the morning and didn't leave his office until late Tuesday evening. Then, he went to a burrito place up the street. We have video of him ordering food, leaving with his order, and entering a nearby hotel a few minutes later. They issued him a keycard for the company suite. There's footage of him and his burrito entering the elevator, then exiting on the floor where the suite is located. We have video of him unlocking the door with the keycard. The door to the suite didn't open again until Wednesday morning. He couldn't have done it."

I tear up, overwhelmed by relief.

"Well…" I sigh. "At least if I go to prison for Paul's murder, Hannah will still have one parent on the outside."

When I hear the words come out of my mouth, I realize they sound glib, but I'm serious. I'm worried because the police haven't eliminated me as a suspect yet, but they've eliminated other people. The suspect list is getting smaller, and my odds of being charged are getting higher.

"As for you,"—Eric hands me another napkin to dab my tears—"you were with Connie until less than ten minutes before you found the body. You are, at best, an unlikely suspect."

I nod. An unlikely suspect, but still a suspect.

"I was planning to tell Adam tomorrow, but we can tell him when I take you home."

I nod. "That would be great, thank you, Eric."

"So, there's no need for you to keep asking questions and putting yourself at risk, right?" he nods at me, looking for agreement.

"Right," I say, nodding back.

Ready to leave, we say goodnight to Sheamus, and head toward the door.

"Thank you for offering to take me home, but you don't have to," I say. "I'll be fine."

"I know," he says, "but it's a good idea for everyone to be extra cautious right now. You know, safety in numbers and all that. Besides, I promised your hus—Adam, and this gives me a chance to tell him he's no longer a suspect."

At the door, I reach for my tote bag to get my lip balm. Where's my tote bag?

"Shoot! My bag. It's under the booth!"

I spot my pumpkin-coloured bag under the table where I left it. I grab it, stride back to Eric, through the door he's holding open, and onto the sidewalk, forgetting about my dry lips and wanting to apply lip balm.

Eric doesn't have a car. He rode with two colleagues who took the car with them when they left. It's a nice evening, so instead of waiting, we decide to walk to my house. He'll text the station and ask for a patrol car to pick him up there.

On the walk to chez Martel, we talk about hockey, we're both Toronto Maple Leafs Fans. We talk about school. I went to U of T, and he went to Western. We talk about TV, we both hate reality shows, I prefer streaming services, he prefers cable. He even answers a few personal questions; he was divorced two years ago. They were married for ten years and she was a chiropractor. His job caused stress in their marriage, and he has no children. He doesn't have a girlfriend because he's married to his job, and when he tries to have a relationship and a career, one suffers, so he gave up trying to have both.

The porch light is on, and the door is locked.

Adam isn't kidding around about our security; we never lock the door when one of us is home. I don't like feeling that I have to lock my door to feel safe in my home.

Instead of ringing the bell and disturbing Adam, I reach into my bag and grope around for my keys. I grab hold of something that feels… odd.

What is this? It's smooth and cylindrical, and Eric and I both watch as I slowly pull a twelve-inch-long, fifteen-millimetre diameter, bamboo knitting needle from my bag and hold it up between us.

"What the f—what is this? This isn't mine. It wasn't in here when I switched bags this morning."

I'm dumbfounded trying to figure out where this knitting needle came from and how it got into my bag.

"Are you sure it's not yours? Maybe it was already in your bag from the last time you used it, and you forgot it was there?"

Eric positions his hands cautiously around the needle, being careful not to touch it, like he's prepared to catch it if it falls.

"I'm sure. We sell these at the shop. In fact, this one is identical to the needles Kelly bought the day Paul died."

I look at his face for a reaction, but he's hyper-focused on the needle I'm dangling between us.

"I don't own needles this big," I explain. "I knit with fingering weight or worsted weight yarn, so my needle collection ranges from about two millimetres to five millimetres. Nothing this big, and I only use circular needles, even when I'm knitting flat. This needle isn't mine."

He looks at me blankly for a second, then returns his focus to the needle.

"I don't know what that means," he says, pressing the doorbell with one hand and guarding the needle with the other. "But this needle might be evidence. I need you to return it carefully to your bag without touching it any more than you already have."

Adam opens the door, looks at me, looks at Eric, then looks at the needle.

"Hey, guys!" he says with a big smile.

CHAPTER 21

HOLDING my bag at arm's length, I hurry from the front door to the dining room and, like it's a grenade instead of a bamboo knitting needle, place the bag on the dining room table. I step away backwards, keeping a watchful eye on it the entire time.

I switch on the dining room light. Eric is behind me on his phone. He requests a car and an evidence kit.

Adam watches the scene with obvious confusion. I tell him about the mysterious knitting needle I found in my bag. He doesn't look any less confused. Adam is used to finding random knitting needles in unexpected places—he's lived with a knitter for almost twenty years—and doesn't think a rogue needle in my tote bag is unusual. I explain this specific needle isn't mine, and Eric thinks it might be evidence. His confused expression morphs into one of concern.

"We have to take the entire bag and its contents for processing," Eric explains when he finishes his call.

"Oh. Can I keep my cell phone? That's the number Hannah uses to reach me."

"Not if it's in your bag, I'm afraid," he responds, shaking his head.

"They'll probably keep it for a while," Adam adds. "They've had my cell phone for almost a week." He snickers. "It might take them a week just to unpack your luggage."

I roll my eyes. Adam always teases me about my love of large tote bags. *Luggage* is one of his many terms of endearment for them. I know he's trying to lighten the mood and ease my anxiety, but I'm not amused.

"It's still early," Adam says, looking at his watch. "I'll go to the store and get you a new phone. You can text Hannah with your new number tonight, and if she needs anything in the meantime, she'll text me or call the landline. We'll tell her the phone got wet or something. It'll be fine."

I nod, sad about lying to my daughter. How would I tell her the police confiscated my cell phone because murder evidence—from a murder

I'm suspected of committing—appeared in my bag?

Adam asks Eric if it's OK for him to leave.

"Go ahead," Eric replies, "but I need to ask you some questions when you get back."

"I'll be as quick as I can."

Adam is already at the door putting on his shoes.

"Can I get you a drink? Coffee or tea or anything?" I go into the kitchen to get myself a glass of water.

Eric stays in the dining room with the tote bag.

"No thanks," he replies. "When was the last time you reached into your bag? Before we got here and you went looking for your keys, I mean."

Retracing my day, I think back. I realized I didn't have my bag when I wanted to put lip balm on as we left the pub. It was under the booth where I put it when I first sat down. I remember wanting my hand sanitizer in the condolence line but forgetting about it because it was my turn to fake-introduce myself to Fred. I didn't need to reach into it for my keys at Knitorious because Connie already unlocked the door.

"When I left the house this afternoon," I shout from the kitchen. "I locked the door and dropped my keys in my bag. I haven't reached into it since. It was on the floor under the booth most of the afternoon. When it wasn't under the booth, it was on my shoulder. I switched bags this morning, and I'm telling you, there were no knitting needles in my bag. Except for the ones that belong in my bag. I have a sock project in there that I work on in line-ups, waiting rooms, you know, when I'm waiting. But it's a sock and has tiny needles."

I remove my boots and put them in the closet. Then I sit on the living room sofa with my feet tucked under my butt. I'm able to position myself with an unobstructed view of the bag.

"Did anyone hold your bag for you?" Eric asks.

"No." I shake my head. "It was on my shoulder or under the booth. Lots of people bumped into it because the pub was so crowded. Are you going to explain why the knitting needle might be evidence?"

"They're here," Eric says, ignoring my question, walking to the front door, and letting in two police officers.

The three law enforcement officers proceed to the dining room, one of them places a black case on the dining room floor. She opens the case, pulls out a pair of latex gloves and puts them on. Then she grabs a large plastic evidence bag, which unfolds into an even larger evidence bag. She reaches into the case again and pulls out smaller evidence bags and lays them in front of her. The other officer reaches into the case and puts latex gloves on. They photograph, bag, and tag the contents of my tote bag. I'm glad Adam isn't here to crack a joke about the size of the evidence bag they need to fit the tote bag inside.

While his colleagues collect the evidence, Eric suggests we wait in another room. I lead him into the family room and resume my tucked-up position on the sofa there. Eric sits at the other end of the sofa.

"Well," I say, "why is this knitting needle potential evidence?"

By instinct, I pick up the sock-in-progress from the ceramic yarn bowl on the table next to me, and start knitting.

"That's a nice bowl. Did you make that?"

I swear this man will do anything to avoid directly answering my questions.

"Thank you. Yes, I took a pottery class a few years ago."

Eric slides closer, so he's in the middle of the sofa instead of the end. He smells good.

"Remember when I explained what a hold-back is?" he asks in a whisper.

"Yes," I whisper, leaning in so I can hear him. "It's evidence only the killer would know about. You keep it secret until you find the killer, then use it to verify their story."

"Pretty much," Eric whispers back. "One of the knitting needles Kelly bought at Knitorious was missing from the crime scene. We can't find it anywhere. We turned the apartment, salon, their cars, everything upside down looking for it. One needle was there, but we never located the other one."

"So, you think the killer took it?" I ask. "Like a sick souvenir or something?"

I cringe at the thought of someone disturbed enough to want a murder memento.

"Possibly," Eric replies with a nod. He pauses, like he's not sure he should say anything else. "The murderer might have used the needle as a garrote. Do you know what a garrote is?"

I look at him and nod. My stomach sinks, and I swallow hard.

A garrote is a weapon used to help strangle someone. The police suspect the killer might have used the knitting needle as a tool to tighten the yarn around Paul's neck. Its sudden appearance in my bag probably means Eric upgraded my status as unlikely suspect to most likely suspect.

"Will you be able to keep the knitting needle a secret, Megan? It would help the investigation if we can keep it under wraps. I know you're close with April and Connie. Will you be able to keep this from them? The killer likely wanted you to find it and touch it, and I'd rather not give this creep what they want." Eric winks.

I give a small smile to his attempt at reassuring me.

I'm not reassured, I'm terrified. My fingerprints are on that needle, I touched it to pull it out of my bag. The killer probably took it with them after they killed Paul, wiped it clean of their own fingerprints, then planted it so I would leave my fingerprints on it. This needle is a direct link between me and Paul's murder.

"Of course, I'll keep it a secret." I tell him firmly.

In silence and with trembling hands, I knit while Eric paces between me and the officers in the dining room.

Adam comes home with my new phone and hands me the box. I take it into the kitchen and plug it in while Eric questions Adam in the family room. The two officers finish collecting the evidence and pack up their things.

I text Hannah with my new number. My mind wanders to the knitting needle while I wait for her to text back an acknowledgement. I touched a weapon that murdered someone. It was in my bag, and I didn't even realize it was there. The murderer got close enough to put it there without raising my suspicion.

A knitting needle, of all things. I love knitting; knitting has brought me comfort during the hardest times of my life, like when my mother passed away. Knitting helped me make friends when we moved to Harmony Lake, and now knitting might frame me for a murder I didn't commit.

I feel gross and dirty and can't wait for the police to leave, so I can lock myself in my room and have a shower.

I STAND under the stream of hot water for I-don't-know-how-long. The tips of my fingers are wrinkled and pruney.

Does Eric believe I'm innocent? Does everyone else believe I'm innocent? Why would the killer want me to find the murder weapon? Why not someone else? Was the murderer at Paul's celebration of life, walking around, acting normal, and doing it so well they didn't stand out?

The water runs cold and I shiver. I turn off the shower and step into the steam-filled washroom to dry off.

I put on my favourite flannel pyjamas with cats and yarn balls on them, a pair of thick, hand-knit, wool socks, and go to the kitchen to make a mug of chamomile tea.

Adam is at the kitchen table with his laptop open.

"Did you text your new number to Hannah?" he asks without looking up from the screen.

"Yes, it's all good," I reply. "Thank you for replacing my phone."

Choking up, I swallow the lump in my throat.

"Do you think I killed Paul?" I blurt out.

My eyes fill with tears, and I can't stop them from streaming down my face.

Adam gets up from the table, picks up a tissue box, and pulls out a couple of tissues. He hands them to me and places the box on the counter next to me.

"I know you didn't kill anybody, Meg," he says. "No one who has ever met you could think you're capable of murder. The killer must feel cornered and desperate to redirect the investigation," he theorizes, rubbing circles into my back. "Eric seems like a thorough investigator who's good at his job. I'm sure he's seen this before. He knows you didn't do it, and he'll find the monster who did."

Adam puts his arms around me, and I let him. I cry there for a while. At least if I'm charged with Paul's murder, I'll have one of the best lawyers around.

After I pull myself together, I make my tea and say goodnight to Adam.

"Eric spoke to you about keeping the knitting needle secret, right?" Adam asks. "It's important, Meg. If we tell anyone, it could jeopardize the investigation." His voice is slow and gentle, like he's trying to reason with a disappointed child.

"I understand," I assure him. "I won't say anything. And I can keep a secret, you know. I've kept our separation a secret for months." As soon as

I say it, I realize I sound bitter, which isn't my intention. "Eric told me he eliminated you as a suspect. He said he was going to tell you tonight," I tell Adam in case Eric forgot to mention it amidst all the commotion.

"He told me," Adam responds. "And I know you can keep a secret, Meg. I also know you confide in your friends. You can't confide in them about this. Tell them the same story about your phone you told Hannah. It'll be easier to keep track of the lies if we keep them consistent," he says, smiling at me. "Goodnight."

He sits down at the kitchen table and resumes working on his laptop.

I've become a person who has so many lies, she has to keep track of them. I need to solve this murder, so I don't have to lie anymore.

This isn't who I am.

CHAPTER 22

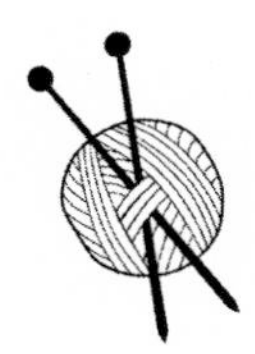

THURSDAY, September 19th

I didn't sleep well. I dreamed I was in prison with the cast of "Orange Is the New Black."

After tossing and turning most of the night, I'm wide awake. I may as well get dressed and go to Knitorious. There are online orders to ship, and I can finish the fall window display.

Realizing the police confiscated my keys with my bag last night, I retrieve the spare set from the hook on the laundry room wall and drive to the store.

Making as little noise as possible, I let myself in the back door. I don't use the front door because the bell might wake up Connie, and no one should be up this early.

Harlow runs downstairs and purrs while he

wraps himself around my ankles. I pick him up, scratch under his chin, tell him how charming he is, and carry him into the store. I sit on a sofa, and he jumps onto my lap. He purrs while I stroke him, and we enjoy some quiet time together until he purrs himself to sleep.

I pick up the cowl I'm working on and knit for a while before I print the online orders. The clicking of the needles and Harlow's purring are the only sounds in the otherwise silent store. For the first time since Paul's murder, anxiety loosens its grip on me. I'm thankful for the reprieve, even if only for a few minutes.

Harlow wakes up, licks himself, and leaps off my lap. He meows and looks back and forth between me and the kitchenette.

"Are you hungry, handsome?" I ask the tuxedo cat.

I stand up, and he runs to the kitchenette. While I dole out Harlow's pungent food, footsteps thud on the steps behind me that lead to Connie's apartment.

"Good morning, sleepy head!" I greet Connie without turning around.

I place the cat dish on the floor and turn toward the stairs.

"Oh!" I gasp, "Where's Connie?"

"Good morning, Megan!" Archie replies.

"Connie will be down in a minute. We didn't think you were coming in this morning,"

This is awkward. For both of us. I had no idea Connie and Archie were more than friends. Does her relationship with Archie have anything to do with Connie's mystery appointments?

Archie and I act like it's the most normal thing in the world for me to catch him doing a walk of shame from Connie's apartment on a Thursday morning.

"How are you doing, Archie? How's the sore hip been treating you?" I hold up a coffee mug to offer him a cup of coffee.

"It's stiff, but as long as I keep using it, it's OK." He shakes his head and waves away my silent coffee offer. "It seizes up when I stop using it, so I try to keep it moving." After an awkward silence he adds, "Listen, Megan, I was talking with Connie, and Ryan might have misinformed you about where he was the night Paul died."

"I wondered about that," I admit, turning on the coffeemaker.

"Well, we watched the game together. That part is true," Archie confesses. "But before that, he wasn't with his friend Jay, he was with me. You caught him off guard, and he didn't know what to say. He was protecting me as much as he was protecting himself."

"Just tell her, Archie!" Connie is coming

downstairs, and this morning-after scene is getting more awkward.

"Good morning, my dear." Connie and I hug, and she kisses my cheek. "Stop beating around the bush, Archie, and tell her where you were," she says, taking his hand.

Archie takes a deep breath.

"Ryan and I were at an AA meeting at a church in Harmony Hills. He got his three-year chip that night."

"Archie, I had no idea!" I say. "Good for him. Tell Ryan I'm proud of him. Sobriety isn't easy. And please tell him his secret is safe with me. I won't tell a soul," I reassure him.

"Us," Archie corrects me. "We were both at the meeting, Megan. I've been sober for 23 years." He smiles at me and then at Connie. "Like father, like son," Archie continues, "I'm afraid my rugged good looks and seductive charm aren't the only things I passed down to my son."

Connie laughs and puts her spare hand on his shoulder.

"Ryan was taken aback when you asked him where he was," Archie explains. "He didn't want to out my sobriety. That's why he lied to you. He feels awful for lying. But he was with me the entire night, I swear."

"I'm proud of both of you." I hug him. "And I couldn't be happier for you and Connie. I feel better knowing you're staying here while there's a killer roaming around Harmony Lake."

I finish making my coffee, say goodbye to Archie and go into the shop to print the online orders. Connie and Archie say goodbye at the back door, then she joins me.

Connie looks happy. She has a glow about her and a spring in her step I haven't seen since her husband passed away five years ago. Archie obviously makes her happy, and that's enough to make me happy for them.

"I mean it, you know," I say. "I'm happy for you and Archie. But why the secrecy?"

"It's not a secret," Connie replies. "We just didn't announce it. We decided to live our life and let people figure it out for themselves. Making a big deal out of it at our age is exhausting, to be honest, and as soon as the right people figure it out, it'll be common knowledge, anyway." She shrugs.

Still smiling, Connie tidies the yarn on the shelves behind the sofa.

I process the online orders and think about what Connie said about her relationship with Archie becoming common knowledge. Until last week, I thought nothing could stay secret in Harmony Lake, but now I realize no matter how small and tight knit our cozy little community is, secrets lurk everywhere, everyone has one. Even our family has a secret, and if we can keep a separation secret for months, anyone can do it. It makes me feel like I don't know my friends and neighbours as well as I thought.

THE FAMILIAR JINGLE makes Connie and me look up at the same time. April strides in with a deep frown.

"There you are!" she shouts, narrowing her eyes on me, and crossing her arms in front of her chest. "I've been texting you all day. I worried, so I texted Adam to make sure you were OK. He said you have a new phone number, and I'd probably find you here. What happened to your phone, and why are you working on your day off?"

"What's this about a new number, my dear?" Connie adds, the skin around her eyes creased with concern.

"I'm sorry! I meant to text you my new number, but I don't *know* your phone numbers. I depend on technology and don't have anyone's contact information memorized or written anywhere." April and Connie continue staring at me, waiting for more of an explanation. "The phone is no big deal, I dropped it in water last night, and it didn't recover. I worried Hannah wouldn't be able to reach me, so Adam replaced it." I make a mental note to get one of those old-timey phone books and write down important numbers, in case the police ever confiscate my phone again.

I smile and look back and forth from April to Connie, hoping they believe me and hating that I just lied to them. Not telling them something is hard enough, but this is an outright lie.

"And?" April prods. "Why are you here? It's your day off."

"There are online orders to process, we need to finish the fall window display, and honestly, home is awkward right now with my soon-to-be-ex-husband there."

The last part isn't a lie, it is awkward having Adam at home so much. We're always in each other's space.

Connie walks over to the counter with her right hand extended, palm-up, and wiggles her fingers. "Give me your phone. I'll text myself, so we have each other's numbers." I hand her my unlocked phone. "I agree with April," Connie adds, "I would've panicked if I tried to reach you and couldn't. We still have a killer roaming around, remember?"

Despite claiming she understands nothing technological, Connie finds the text app, texts herself, and hands the phone back to me, with no help or tech support. I hold the phone out to April, who takes it and adds her and Tamara's numbers.

"Why were the police at your house?" April

asks. "Phillip said two patrol cars were there for quite a while."

Uh-oh. Adam and I didn't come up with a lie to explain why the police were there. I wonder if Phillip saw the police leave with evidence bags?

"Eric walked me home after the wake, and his colleagues came to pick him up."

It's not an outright lie. I know I'm lying by omission, but it feels less awful than saying something completely untrue.

"Phillip said there were two cars," April says, holding up two fingers, "Eric needs two cars to drive him around?" She raises her eyebrows and tilts her head.

She's not buying it. April knows me too well. Connie stands next to her in some kind of show of solidarity, crossing her arms in front of her chest.

"Ok, Eric needed a ride back to the station, that's true. He also told Adam that they eliminated him as a suspect. And... he called his colleagues to pick up.... some.... evidence...that appeared suddenly last night."

"Keep talking, my dear," Connie says, moving her hand in a rolling motion in front of her.

"I want to tell you, but I can't," I blurt out. "Eric said it would compromise the investigation. Please stop asking because I want to tell you, but I can't. And please don't mention it to anyone." I bring my palms together in a pleading motion in front of my face.

"Of course, we won't say anything! We know you'd tell us if you could. Let's just hope whatever it is, it breaks the case wide open and gets this murderer off our streets."

"Your secrets are always safe with us, my dear." Connie says as she wraps her arms around both of us and gives us a tight squeeze.

"Now that we've sorted that out," April says, "Latte Da's fall menu starts today and I'm craving a spiced caramel apple latte. Come with me to see the other fall yummies they added to their menu this year." April rubs her tummy in a circular motion.

As much as I love coffee, April loves it more. Her commitment to caffeine is admirable. Coffee is kind of her hobby.

"Give me five minutes to pack this order, so I can drop these off at the post office on our way." I gesture to the pile of packaged orders on the counter.

I place the packaged orders into a large reusable laundry bag with a pink and brown tartan pattern.

"That laundry bag is almost as big as your purse!" April says, pointing at the large bag, laughing, and looking at Connie who's covering her mouth with her hand to hide her laughter.

"Ha! Ha!" I say, "Everyone likes to make fun of

my bag until they need me to carry something for them, don't they, April?"

I shoot April a sideways glance without lifting my head. April only carries a wristlet which acts as her phone case and wallet, so whenever we go anywhere together, she puts whatever doesn't fit in her wristlet—which is basically everything—in my tote. At any given time, half the contents in my bag belong to her.

My cell phone dings.

Adam: Can you meet me at 845 Mountain Road at 1pm? I want to show you something.

Me: Yes! C u there!

I'm so excited, I almost add a smiley emoji to the end of my text reply.

"I don't want to jinx it, but I think Adam found an apartment," I say. "I overheard him on the phone the other day. It sounded like he was arranging a viewing. He just texted me to meet him at 845 Mountain Road at 1 p.m."

I'm grinning so wide my cheeks hurt, and I do a little happy dance behind the counter.

"Mountain Road...those are older houses, right? Some converted to duplexes and triplexes, I think? And a few renovated as offices? A bit off the beaten path, but nice and close to the highway." April nods.

"That reminds me." Connie snaps her fingers and interjects, "I have an appointment tomorrow, late morning. Will you be OK by yourself for a couple of hours?"

"Of course," I tell her. "Is everything OK, Connie? You've had several appointments over the last few weeks, should we worry?"

Scared the answer might be yes, I brace myself. Connie is like a mother to me, and I can't imagine anything happening to her. Sure, she's slowing down a bit, but she's still the healthiest, most active senior I know.

"Nothing to worry about, my dear." She waves her hand dismissively. "At my age a few extra appointments are to be expected," she adds with a reassuring wink.

"Promise you'd tell us if something was wrong?" April extends her pinky finger to Connie for a pinky swear, and Connie, hooking her own pinky finger around April's, says, "pinky swear, my dear."

CHAPTER 23

April and I move our sunglasses from the tops of our heads to our eyes in unison as we step onto the sunny sidewalk. We walk toward Latte Da, enjoying the sun on our faces while I tell her Ryan is off their suspect list. I'm careful not to disclose where Ryan and Archie were when Paul was murdered. I worry she might press for details about Ryan's alibi, but lucky for me, she forgets all about Ryan when I tell her I caught Archie leaving Connie's apartment this morning.

"Just wow!" April's mouth hangs open in disbelief. "I mean, good for them. They deserve to be happy. It's shocking how we live in such a small town, and are so close with Connie, yet we never knew."

"I know," I agree with her. "I've been thinking

the same thing lately. We assume because Harmony Lake is so tiny and everybody knows one another, that it's hard to keep a secret, but since Paul died, all we've done is find out people's secrets. It makes me wonder how well we really know anyone."

"Well, you know me!" April pulls the door and motions for me to go ahead of her. "I have no secrets. What you see is what you get."

She lets the door close behind her and joins me in line. Latte Da is busy today. Everyone is checking out the fall menu and ordering their favourite fall drinks they haven't had since last fall.

We order our coffees and sit at the only available table. I put my mocha chip iced coffee on the table, settle into my seat and pull out my knitting. I want to finish Hannah's cowl and hat before she comes home for Thanksgiving in a few weeks. Hopefully Eric will solve Paul's murder by then, and Hannah won't come home to a mother who is a murder suspect. Thinking about Hannah and what could happen if the police don't find Paul's killer makes me tearful. I swallow hard, fighting the urge to cry.

"Hey..." April touches my knee. "Are you OK? You aren't listening to my review of this Spiced Caramel Apple Latte, or is it so boring it's bringing you to tears?"

"I'm sorry," I drop my knitting in my lap. "Hannah will be home for Thanksgiving in three weeks, and I'm still a murder suspect. We haven't even told her about the investigation. She has no idea I'm a suspect, or that Adam was a suspect. I just want it solved so badly."

A familiar voice gets my attention, and I look toward the cash register where Kelly is paying for her order. Hairway to Heaven is next door, so I'm not surprised to run into her here. Kelly looks over and our eyes meet. She waves.

"Hey ladies!" she calls. "Save me a seat. I'll join you when Gingerbread Spiced Coffee is ready."

We wave back and nod.

"I still have feelings about her knowing about Adam and Stephanie and not saying anything," I whisper to April.

"I get it," April whispers, "but Stephanie is her sister. You're like my sister, and I wouldn't rat you out if you had an affair. Even if she told you, would it have changed anything? You and Adam were splitting up, anyway. The affair was still a threat to Adam's career. And you both would have wanted the text messages and photos kept private. It wouldn't have changed anything."

"You're right," I agree, "but it sucks to feel like I can't trust her. And she's such a good liar."

I sit up and move my large, cinnamon-coloured tote from the chair between April and me to the chair on my other side. As Kelly walks over, I pat the empty chair, motioning for her to sit down.

Kelly sits, puts her drink on the table, her purse

on the floor, and sighs. I smile at her. Convincing liar or not, if she didn't kill Paul, Kelly needs all the support she can get right now.

She looks tired and wears less makeup than usual. Her hair is in a low ponytail instead of the full blow out she usually dons when she's working. Her only jewelry is her wedding band and a pair of delicate, gold love-knot earrings.

"Those earrings are lovely," April says, as if reading my mind.

April excels at small talk, a quality I admire and am grateful for because her gift for gab has saved me from an awkward silence more than once.

"Thank you. They were a gift from my grandparents when I was a teenager. They gave us each an identical pair,"—Kelly gestures toward the counter where Stephanie is paying for a drink—"but she has a metal allergy and can't wear any jewelry. None. No gold, no silver, nothing. She breaks out in a horrible rash that lasts for days if she even touches the stuff."

Trying not to react to Stephanie's presence, I move my tote bag from the chair beside me to the floor to make room for her.

"Listen, ladies, thanks for coming to Paul's celebration of life yesterday," Kelly says, putting one hand on my lap and her other hand on April's lap. "I wish I could've spent more time with you, but it was busy, and overwhelming. I'm not sure I even talked to everyone once."

April puts her hand on Kelly's hand, which is on her knee. "How was your first night at home?"

"Not good." Kelly shakes her head. "Much harder than I expected." She perks up. "Stephanie! Over here!" she waves until Stephanie notices her and waves back.

I give April a look that says, *Really? We're going to have coffee with Stephanie and pretend we're all friends?*

In return, April shoots me a look I interpret as, *I know, just grin and bear it for Kelly.*

"I thought it would be comforting to go home," Kelly explains, "with all our stuff and happy memories. But I was an emotional mess. I ended up calling Stephanie. She came and stayed with me."

"That's understandable," I say. "It's only been a week, you're still in shock, and maybe until the police arrest the mur—person, it's safer to not be alone, anyway."

"Look, Megan, before Stephanie comes over..." The three of us glance toward the counter. Stephanie is still waiting for her coffee. "I'm sorry I didn't tell you about her and Adam. I didn't know until after Paul died. The day before he died, she told me she was seeing someone, but she didn't tell me who it was. I found out during the investigation."

"I understand," I say, nodding. "You were in an awful position."

Kelly's version of events matches what Fred told me outside the pub yesterday.

"But, even if I knew,"—Kelly shrugs—"she's my sister. I don't think I would have told you. I hated knowing, and I hope this doesn't hurt our friendship."

Kelly places her hand on my knee again. Her big, sorrowful eyes are full of sincerity.

"Did you know Fred and Stephanie used the photos to blackmail Adam into leaving the firm? So, Stephanie could stay there without Fred having to worry about her and Adam working together?" I ask.

There isn't time to gauge Kelly's reaction because Stephanie is on her way to the table. We all plaster smiles to our faces.

"Hi ladies," Stephanie mutters, looking down at her drink.

"Hi," April and I say weakly in unison.

To distract myself from Stephanie's presence, and obsessing over what the heck Adam saw in her, I pick up my cowl and resume knitting.

"Is the salon open again?" April asks, fussing with her bangs.

"Yes," Kelly replies. "My stylists need to work. They worried their clients might go elsewhere if we didn't open again. And it's good for me to keep busy."

"Kelly will work at the salon during the day," Stephanie adds, "and at night she'll stay with us." Stephanie smiles at her sister. "She knows there's always a room for her at our house."

"It's amazing how well I sleep at Stephanie and Fred's house," Kelly says wistfully. "Every night, within an hour of eating supper, I'm so relaxed and drowsy that I take myself off to bed, and the next thing I know, it's morning. Stephanie and our mom think it's all the crying and emotions. Grief is exhausting."

"You're lucky to have each other," I say. "So how's Fred doing?"

I couldn't care less about Fred; I'm trying to do my part in this awkward, painful conversation. I take a sip of my iced coffee.

"He's been so great!" Kelly says. "He's upstairs right now, packing an overnight bag. I couldn't cope with going into the apartment today. Fred and Stephanie are making sure I don't have to."

"I think he's packing the car." Stephanie looks behind her, "He said he'll pop in to let us know when everything's packed, and we can head out."

April fusses with her bangs again. "No pressure, Kelly, but when you have time, I'd love to see you for a bang trim, and maybe you could clean up my ends? There's no rush, I won't go anywhere else. Whenever you're ready."

"I think I can squeeze you in tomorrow, hun! Let's pop next door so I can look at my schedule." Kelly stands up, grabs her drink, and gestures for April to follow her.

Next thing I know, they're both gone and I'm alone with Stephanie, pretending this isn't the most uncomfortable situation of my life.

"Well, this is awkward," Stephanie states the obvious.

"What? Having coffee with my husband's girlfriend?" I shrug. "Just another Thursday, Stephanie."

My words drip with sarcasm, and I don't care. I sip my iced coffee and resume knitting while sending telepathic messages to April telling her to hurry up.

Stephanie clears her throat. "I'm not his g—," she starts with a meek, wimpy voice.

"Girlfriend?" I finish her sentence for her. "You and Adam agree on that. Neither of you want you referred to as *Adam's girlfriend*."

I smile and look around for another free table, hoping I can move, alone. Nothing. Latte Da's new fall menu is a big event in Harmony Lake, and all the tables are full of people enjoying their beverages and the company of friends and neighbours. Except our table. There's no enjoyment at our table. *Please come back, April.*

"Megan, I'm sorry. I never intended to interfere in your marriage. I regret the affair. I wish it never happened."

I don't buy Stephanie's attempt at a heartfelt apology. Her forced sincerity is fake and patronizing.

"So, the affair wasn't part of your blackmail scheme from the beginning?" I ask.

It's crossed my mind more than once that blackmailing Adam was Stephanie's goal all along. Adam's departure from the firm creates an opportunity for everyone below him to move up a rung on the career ladder, including Stephanie.

"No," Stephanie says with her feeble voice, shaking her head. "There was no scheme. It was a mistake. Adam is charming and handsome, and I was weak."

Sneaky, sneaky Stephanie. I see what you're doing. You're subtly branding Adam as the pursuer and minimizing your own role in this mess. I'm thinking Stephanie is a skilled manipulator who hides behind her meek, shy persona act.

"I didn't want to blackmail anyone. That was all Fred," She looks down at her drink. "But I didn't stop him."

I'm not a lawyer, but I know Stephanie just admitted to aiding and abetting a crime. Blackmail is a crime, and Stephanie, aware that it was happening, didn't stop it or report it. She's a lawyer, for goodness' sake, an officer of the court. We both know I won't say anything. It would be her word against mine; nothing will come from her admission.

"Adam is a senior partner. He has a well-established career and reputation. It's much easier for him to find a new position than for me. I'm a newer lawyer and junior associate. I love Fred and want our marriage to work, but Fred can't move past the affair if Adam and I work together. I truly am sorry for everything, and I hope your marriage survives this as well."

Stephanie gives me a meek smile and looks down at her cup. I put my knitting on my lap and lean toward her.

"I'm telling you this for one reason," I hiss, trying to whisper and control my anger. "You and your blackmailing husband have no influence over my life. None." Squinting, I focus my gaze into her eyes. "Adam and I separated months before you and he swapped dirty text messages and photos. You did not destroy our marriage. Because *you aren't significant enough.* Your six-week affair didn't end our twenty-year marriage, years of apathy and disinterest did. You aren't even a blip on the radar of my life. You came along after our marriage ended. And knowing Adam as well as I do, you were just a distraction." I sneer, shaking my head.

I snatch my tote bag from the floor and drop my knitting into it. Then I stand up, throw my bag over my shoulder, grab my coffee, and stride to the door without looking back.

CHAPTER 24

SQUINTING INTO THE HARSH DAYLIGHT, I slide my sunglasses from the top of my head to my eyes and get my bearings as I swallow the last of my mocha chip iced coffee.

I dump my empty coffee cup in a nearby recycling receptacle and keep walking. I'm about to text April to explain why I bolted from Latte Da when my left shoulder bumps into someone walking toward me. When I look up to apologize, Fred Murphy is looking down at me.

It feels like the Murphys are everywhere I go today. I acknowledge Fred with a curt nod and continue on my way. Determined to as far away as possible from the Murphys, I pick up the pace as I go.

I'm in the alley beside Knitorious, almost at my car, when my phone dings from inside my bag.

Inside the car, I lock the door because, on top of everything else that happened this week, I've become someone who locks her car and house to feel safe, even when she's in them.

I plug my phone into the console and check my texts. Adam. We were just talking about him. I bet his ears are burning, as my mother used to say when someone she was thinking or talking about would call or show up.

Adam: Where are you? Everything OK?

I start the car and look at the time on the dashboard: 1:05 p.m. I'm late.

Me: On my way. Be there in 10.

On the short drive to Mountain Road, I contemplate how the Stephanie I met at Paul's wake and the Stephanie today at Latte Da are like different people. Which version of Stephanie Murphy is real and which one is fake?

Since learning about Adam and Stephanie's affair, I've wondered who made the first move. Fred said Stephanie made the first move, but after meeting meek and mousey yesterday-Stephanie, I couldn't imagine her making a first move to get anything, and figured Adam was more likely the pursuer. But after talking to today-Stephanie, I'm considering a third possibility: she chased him until he caught her. Stephanie let Adam believe the relationship was his idea, but she was in charge the entire time. Passive aggressive and manipulative.

I'm also not convinced Stephanie sent Adam's photo to her husband by accident. Maybe it was a calculated move to expose the affair and eliminate Adam as an obstacle on her career path.

845 Mountain Road is a large, Victorian-era house. I park on the road and sit in the car, assessing my surroundings. Mountain Road is in one of the oldest areas of Harmony Lake. The lots are large, with stately houses set far back from the road. Mature, leafy trees and tall, imposing coniferous trees punctuate the large front yards.

Several houses have signs indicating they're now duplexes, triplexes, or professional buildings. The neighbourhood predates sidewalks, and old-fashioned lamp posts connected by electrical wires line the east side of the road. During tourist season, Mountain Road is busy with tourists coming and going from the two vacation resorts in the mountains; skiers in the winter, and city-escapees in the summer.

I text Adam and let him know I'm outside. I exit the car and lock the door, listening for the chirp.

As I approach the wraparound porch, the large front door opens with Adam on the other side, waving. With a wide grin, he bounces on his heels and beckons me inside. He's downright giddy.

Adam hasn't been this excited since he made senior partner at the firm.

One step inside and I can tell right away this house wasn't converted to residential apartments. It was renovated into office suites. I try to hide my disappointment and not ruin Adam's obvious joy. Hopefully, he's wrapped up in his own excitement and doesn't notice my initial shock that this isn't his new home.

What was originally a grand foyer is now a reception area. The sitting area has a leather sofa, two leather chairs, a coffee table, and two end tables with magazines and brochures fanned out.

To my left is an ornate, wooden reception desk and coat rack that look like they were custom made to match the restored ornate woodwork of the railings, banisters, and moldings throughout the house.

Behind the desk, a young woman smiles and waves while answering the phone. Her black hair almost camouflages her hands-free headset. When she ends her call, Adam introduces us. Her name is Lin Chow. She's friendly and has kind eyes.

Lin offers me a refreshment, which I decline. Then, Adam takes me on a tour of the main floor; meeting rooms, a kitchen, two washrooms, and a supply room with printers, a fax machine, boxes of paper, shredders, and office supplies. Exactly what you'd expect to find in a professional building.

We climb the wooden staircase, and at the end of the hall, on the right, we enter Adam's future office. It's already furnished in the same ornate-wood theme that was prevalent on the main floor. I look around and decide it's professional and lawyerly. A very Adam-like office.

Adam tells me his professional neighbours are an accountant, an insurance broker, a financial planner, and a psychologist who specializes in relationship and family counseling.

Despite my disappointment that he won't be living at 845 Mountain Road, I do my best to join in Adam's excitement, and decide against telling him about my interaction with Stephanie Murphy. He's happier and more hopeful than he has been in ages, and I don't want to ruin it.

We FaceTime Hannah and give her a tour too. When we end our video call, I notice it's almost 2:30 p.m.

"Shoot! I have to get going," I say. "I need to get to the bank and hardware store before they close."

I need to replace my bank card and get another set of keys cut. Since I have no idea if or when the police will return the contents of my bag, I need to replace my stuff.

"I'll walk you out," Adam says as we leave his new office. I say goodbye to Lin and tell her it was nice to meet her. "Congratulations on your new office, it's great," I say to Adam on the porch.

"Thanks. I'll see you at home after your errands."

With an air of vigilance, Adam stands guard on the porch while I walk to my car, lock myself inside, and drive off.

Seeing how concerned he is about our safety is making me paranoid that I'm not concerned enough. Was the knitting needle a warning that I would be next? I shudder at the thought. When I arrive at the bank, I park in a metered spot on the visible, well populated street in front of the bank, instead of parking for free in the secluded parking lot behind it. Changing my routine because of this situation makes me sad, but maybe right now, safety is more important than my feelings.

CHAPTER 25

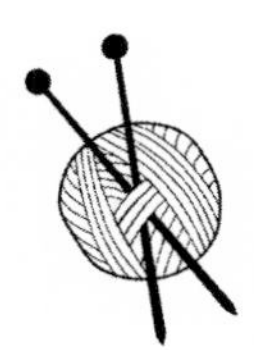

Ryan Wright is kneeling on the front porch, changing the lock on the front door. Why is he here?

"Hey, Ryan!" I smile. "Whatcha doin'?"

"Hey, Megan." He pauses his work to talk to me. "Adam asked me to come over and re-key the house. So, here I am." He smiles and shrugs.

"Oh, he didn't mention it."

I try to control the tone of my voice, so it won't give away how annoyed I am. *Thanks for talking to me about the new locks, Adam!*

"Listen, Ryan, I'm sorry I questioned your alibi, and I'm sorry if I made you feel like a murder suspect. I spoke with your Dad, and he cleared things up," I say, and gently touch his arm. "Also, congratulations on your three-year chip. I'm proud of you, and I promise your secret is safe with me. I'd never disclose it to anybody."

"I know you won't say anything, Megan." Ryan smiles. "I'm not ashamed of being a recovering alcoholic, but my livelihood depends on people being comfortable enough to let me into their homes and businesses. Near their families. Some people would think twice if they knew about my past… issues."

"You'll always have work at chez Martel! We're useless at fixing anything. If not for you and Archie, we'd have to sit on boxes of flat-packed, unassembled furniture, surrounded by drippy faucets and broken appliances," I joke. Sort of.

I walk past Ryan and into the house. Adam is speaking to someone. I assume he's on the phone and try to make as little noise as possible. Entering the kitchen, I see that he isn't on the phone; he's at the kitchen table on his computer, talking to the empty room.

"Oscar, stop!" Adam says when he sees me.

"OK, transcription stopped," Oscar responds.

"It's a transcription app," Adam explains. "Instead of typing a letter, or email, or whatever, I dictate to the app, and it emails a transcript to me. Then I can forward the transcript to my legal secretary who can clean it up and format it."

"That's cool," I reply, "It sounds like a real time-saver."

I'm still annoyed about Adam having the locks changed without discussing it with me first.

"Why is Ryan changing the locks?" I ask, trying to sound non-confrontational.

"Because yesterday a killer accessed your purse and everything in it, including the keys to our home," Adam justifies.

That means they also had access to the keys to Knitorious. I should've made this connection sooner. I make a mental note to ask Ryan to re-key Knitorious.

"You should have discussed it with me first, since I live here too. In fact, I'm supposed to be the only one who lives here. We had a plan, Adam. You said you'd find somewhere to live this month, not find office space. Have you even looked for an apartment?"

"I'm not moving out until the police arrest Paul's murderer," he replies matter-of-factly.

"What if the police never arrest Paul's killer?" I ask. "What if this turns into one of those cold cases?" Frustration seeps into my voice despite my best efforts to stop it.

"Meg, I'm not budging on this," Adam insists. "We might not be together anymore, but you're still my wife. You'll always be Hannah's mother, and we'll always be family. I have to protect my family. I'm not moving out while a killer roams around town, rummaging around in your purse whenever they feel like it. If you want to deny the seriousness of the situation, that's fine. But you and your denial should get used to having me as a roommate. At least until the police solve this murder and the killer is behind bars."

Seething with anger, I clench my jaw muscles so hard they hurt. Adam decided all of this without talking to me. And on top of everything else, he's using his condescending lawyer voice. I hate when he uses his lawyer voice to argue with me.

"Again, *Adam*." I emphasize his name in the most condescending tone of voice I can summon, my version of his lawyer voice. "I'm an adult with the right to make my own decisions. Including whether we change the locks and whether we continue to live under the same roof. Maybe *I* should move out and *you* should stay here."

It's an empty threat. I'd never leave my home. It's more my home than Adam's, and he knows it. I chose every piece of furniture, tchotchke, and paint colour. I clean it, maintain it inside and out, and have spent countless nights and weekends alone inside it, raising Hannah, while Adam was elsewhere, focusing on his career.

"Don't be so dramatic, Meg!"

He did *not* just call me dramatic!

"This house is big enough for both of us," Adam argues. "We can co-exist a while longer without getting in each other's way."

"You're dismissing my feelings, Adam!" I growl out of frustration. "Stop doing that!" I shout.

"OK, transcription stopped," Oscar says, interrupting my tirade.

We look at the small device on the end table. Oscar's light changes colour from yellow to blue, and Adam and I look at each other.

"He recorded our argument?" I ask, pointing at Oscar, "and emailed it to you?" I ask, pointing at Adam's laptop.

"Maybe," Adam says, swiping his fingers across the track pad on his laptop to wake it up. Staring at the screen, he types on the keyboard. "Sure did!" he confirms. "I just got an email of our conversation starting when I said, *I'm not moving out the police arrest Paul's murderer.* Before that, one of us must've said something that triggered the dictation app."

I try to recall what we said that could have triggered Oscar, but it's a jumble of raised voices and hurt feelings. Oscar probably said something like, "Dictation started," but we didn't hear it over our shouting.

As if I need another reason to solve this murder. Adam's determination to live here until the killer is behind bars just rocketed to the top of the list.

"That's creepy. Have you received emails of our conversations before?" I ask.

"No," he replies without looking away from his

laptop screen, "but I only installed the app a few days ago. Maybe I should delete it."

We're interrupted by a knock at the door.

"Ryan," we say in stereo.

"I totally forgot he was here," I comment on my way to answer it.

"Sorry to interrupt." Ryan cranes his neck, moving his head from side-to-side. He's trying to look past me into the house, probably to see what all the shouting is about. "Here are your keys."

He dangles two keys and two business cards between his thumb and forefinger.

I open my hand and Ryan drops the keys and cards into it. The business cards have a seven-digit code on the back. Seeing my confusion, Ryan explains that Adam upgraded to smart locks. *Of course, he did!* And he didn't discuss it with me first, either. We can lock and unlock the house with a key, a phone app, or by talking to Oscar.

"Do you want me to demonstrate?" Ryan offers.

I'm not interested in downloading another app, so I decline Ryan's offer and silently resolve to continue locking and unlocking the doors the old-school way, with a key.

Before he leaves, I ask Ryan if he can change the locks at Knitorious, too, since the store keys were also on my missing key ring. He tells me he's leaving today for an out-of-town job until Monday night. In the meantime, his dad will install an extra lock on the inside of both doors. Ryan says he'll meet me at the store first thing Tuesday morning and re-key both locks.

I give one of the business cards with the code on it to Adam, but don't give him a key. He won't be living here much longer anyway, I reason, so he can use the app.

I retrieve the spare key we keep hidden under the mat on the back deck and replace it with a new key Ryan gave me. When I come back in the house, Adam is staring at me.

"You won't use it anyway," I say. "You love technology. You'll only use the app."

He flips the business card over and uses his cell phone to scan the code, so he can download the app and set it up on his phone.

"Did you know the app works anywhere in the world?" Adam asks, super excited about his new tech toy. "If we leave the country, we can still lock and unlock the house. And we can set it so the door locks automatically thirty seconds after it closes."

I text Hannah and tell her I misplaced my keys and send her the code and app info.

CHAPTER 26

FRIDAY, September 20th

When I arrive at Knitorious, I'm relieved to find that—just like Ryan said—Archie installed a brand-new, shiny barrel-lock on both doors.

Connie invites me for a sleepover after work, and I accept. We haven't had a sleepover in ages, and I'm looking forward to the break from Adam.

After a yummy spaghetti Bolognese dinner, we apply face masks that, according to the packaging, will make us look ten years younger. Then we eat too many chocolate-covered almonds and drink wine while we binge-watch a new-to-us show. It's about three suburban homemakers who hold up a grocery store to solve their financial problems and end up working with in international money laundering ring. Hijinks and hilarity ensue.

Lying in the silence and darkness of Connie's spare room with Harlow purring next to my head, I'm more relaxed than I have been in days and welcome a good night's sleep.

SATURDAY, September 21st

The store is busy, which helps the day pass quickly. Life is returning to normal in Harmony Lake. There's no more crime scene tape, the salon is open for business as usual, and Paul's murder is consuming less of the town's collective consciousness. Paul's murder is still the hottest discussion topic in town. But between concocting theories about Paul's murder, people are talking about other things again. By the way, the latest theory is Paul's murder was a professional hit because he confronted a mob boss for littering.

After work, Connie packs an overnight bag, and she and Harlow leave to spend the rest of the weekend at Archie's place until Ryan can change the locks on Tuesday. I head home to wash, dry, and fold laundry while I watch the second season of the show Connie and I watched last night.

SUNDAY, September 22nd

Adam and I have our weekly FaceTime call with Hannah, and she tells us all about university and life in the big city. We're relieved and happy to see how well she's adjusting to living away from home. She's coping better than us, but she's not embroiled in a police investigation.

I spend some time outside, giving the gardens some much-needed maintenance, then have a shower and go to April and Tamara's house for lunch.

April's cheddar pancetta quiche with thyme is delicious, and Tamara spoils us with homemade chocolate eclairs. They have a knack for making elegant food look easy to prepare, and for making easy to prepare food look elegant. I tell April about my girls' night with Connie and recommend the show we watched. While we're talking, April and Tamara's phones chime.

"It's the WSBA group chat," Tamara says.

"Fred Murphy, Kelly Sinclair's brother-in-law, is missing," April reads. "The police would like anyone with information to contact them. Then it has Eric's number."

"Interesting," I say.

"I bet he did a runner," April surmises. "He killed Paul, and he knows the police are about to arrest him, so he took off." She shrugs her right shoulder.

April believes Fred did it. He's been her number

one suspect since we found out he is Paul and Kelly's brother-in-law.

"If he did it, and now he's on the run, let's hope he's far away from here," Tamara adds. "Someone that desperate might do anything to avoid being caught. And if he already killed once, he has nothing to lose. I hope none of us run into him."

"Me too," I say.

"I wonder how long he's been missing. The last time I saw him was Thursday, after my dramatic exit from Latte Da. He was on the sidewalk."

"I didn't see him on Thursday, but I remember Kelly and Stephanie telling us he was loading the car with Kelly's stuff. They were waiting for him to finish up so they could leave, remember?" April asks, nudging me, and I nod.

"Well, I haven't seen him since I shook his hand at the pub on Wednesday in the condolence line," Tamara adds.

"What if he's not on the run?" I ask. "What if he discovered who killed Paul, and they killed him?"

Since the knitting needle from the murder scene turned up in my bag, I've wondered if the killer was trying to send me a message: stop snooping and stop asking questions.

April and Tamara give me leftovers for Adam, and I somehow manage not to eat his eclair on the drive home.

"April and T sent leftovers for you," I announce,

holding up the glass containers with the quiche and eclair inside. Adam is lounging on the sofa, watching golf. "Do you want them now? Or should I put them in the fridge?"

Adam pauses the TV and comes into the kitchen. He opens the cutlery drawer, grabs a fork, closes the drawer with his hip, takes the rubber lid off the glass container with the quiche. He leans against the counter and eats.

"This is fantastic," Adam says, using his fork to point at the quiche in the container.

"I know, right?" I answer. "Did you hear that Fred Murphy is missing?" I throw it out there without warning.

"No." He shakes without looking up and stabs the quiche with his fork. "Where did you hear that?"

"The WSBA texted the girls about it during lunch."

Adam swallows the last forkful of quiche and puts the container and his fork in the sink. I bite the inside of my lip to stop myself from pointing out that the dishwasher is literally right beside him, next to the sink. Infuriating. Then he reaches for the container with the eclair in it.

"The last time I saw Fred was on Thursday, outside Latte Da, right before I met you at your office. When did you last see him?" I ask.

He turns his back to me and eats the flaky eclair over the sink.

"Wednesday. At the pub. With you," he mumbles with his mouth full and still facing away from me.

We stand in silence for a moment. Adam finishes his éclair and wipes his hands.

"That was good. I'll text the girls and thank them." Then he returns to the family room, resumes the TV, and picks up his phone.

CHAPTER 27

TUESDAY, September 24th

Ryan arrives and gets to work changing the locks as soon as I flip the sign from CLOSED to OPEN and unlock the door. I unpack a yarn order at the counter, trying not to let the random jingle of the bell as Ryan works trick me into looking up.

"Thanks for getting here so fast, Ryan. I'm sure you have a waiting list after leaving town for four days. I appreciate it."

"Anything for family!" he replies.

I look at him confused.

"We're practically family now," he explains. "Archie's my dad and Connie may as well be your mom, so that kind of makes us...step siblings? I think?"

It's his turn to look confused, but he's right.

"So, when does Adam open for business at his new office on Mountain Road?" Ryan asks.

His question takes me by surprise; I didn't realize Adam told anyone about his practice yet. I mentioned it to April and Connie, so maybe Connie told Archie, and Archie told Ryan?

"Sometime next month," I respond. "I didn't realize he mentioned it to you."

"He didn't," Ryan clarifies. "Lin told me. I think he'll enjoy working there. The building is well-maintained. Dad and I do most of the maintenance, so it's quality work." He smiles.

"Did Lin mention it when you were there doing a job?" I ask.

"No, she told me last night." He looks up at me. "Lin and I are dating. We had dinner last night when I got home."

Another secret I've learned this week to add to my ever-growing list.

"Lin and I just started dating. Not very many people know yet."

"Other than April and Connie, I won't say anything," I assure him. "I hope it works out, if that's what you both want, and you're happy together."

"Thanks, Megan." He drops a tool into his toolbox and stands up. "I have to run to my truck for a few minutes. I'll be back."

Ryan hurries through the store and leaves through the back door.

Seconds later, the jingle above the door heralds Eric's arrival.

"Long time no see." I smile, coming out from behind the counter. "Is this a business call or are you taking me up on my offer to teach you how to knit?" I ask, trying to ease the tension in his face.

Eric doesn't appreciate my attempt at humour. His jaw stays firmly clenched and the muscles around his eyes are taut. This is definitely a business call, and whatever brings him here is serious.

"We found Fred Murphy," he says.

I let out a sigh of relief. Why doesn't Eric look relieved?

"Alive?" I ask.

"He was in the back of a rented cube van parked in front of 845 Mountain Road."

Adam's new office! The look on my face must betray my shock because Eric asks if I'm familiar with the address. I sit in a chair in the cozy area.

"Adam rented an office there last week," I explain. "He's not open for business yet, but he showed me around on Thursday."

"Who else knows he rented an office there?" Eric asks, retrieving his trusty notebook and pen from his breast pocket. "And specifically, who knows you were there on Thursday?"

"Hannah," I reply. "We video chatted with her while we were there. Lin, the receptionist. Connie and April. That's it, as far as I know. I'm not sure if Adam has told anyone."

Then I remember!

"Oh! And Ryan Wright. He said Lin told him."

"Is Fred OK?" I need to know. "I mean, he was alive in the back of the cube van, right?"

My short-lived sense of relief disappears with the shake of Eric's head.

In shock, I fidget with my ring while Eric writes in his notebook until the back door thuds, breaking the silence.

"Hey, Detective Sloane," Ryan greets Eric and resumes working on the front door.

"Hello, Mr. Wright," Eric responds. "How are you?"

"I think I'll slip out for a minute and pick up a snack." An excuse to make myself scarce so Eric and Ryan can talk in private. I flip the sign on the door from OPEN to CLOSED. "Would either of you like anything?"

They decline my offer. I leave through the front door and speed walk to Artsy Tartsy.

April is behind the counter serving the only customer in the bakery. I glare at her, wide-eyed. April widens her eyes to match mine and calls for Tamara. Closing the office door behind her, Tamara joins April behind the counter. April finishes cashing out her customer, and we all watch him leave.

Though the bakery is empty, I stand on my tippy toes and lean over the counter. April and Tamara lean toward me until our faces are only inches apart.

"They found Fred," I whisper. "He's dead. He was at Adam's new office. In a rented cube van."

I explain that I can't stay long because I said I was only going to get a snack.

With no time to waste, we brainstorm. Who killed Fred? How did he die? Why did the killer choose the address on Mountain Road? Were they trying to implicate Adam or me? Maybe Fred couldn't live with what he'd done and killed himself. Maybe Fred discovered who the killer was, and they killed him to keep him quiet.

Fred was our number one suspect, and now, defeated, we're back at square one.

"Maybe there are two killers," April suggests. "Maybe Fred killed Paul, and someone murdered Fred to avenge Paul's death."

Her commitment to believing Fred murdered Paul is strong.

"Paul didn't have many friends," Tamara points out. "I can't think of anyone who would kill to avenge his death."

"He has a grieving widow," I remind everyone.

"It wasn't Ryan," I affirm, then tell them about Ryan's out-of-town job.

"Ryan's alibis aren't always rock solid," April reminds me.

"He's dating Lin. Why would he leave a dead body outside her office?" I check the time on my phone while April and Tamara process the news about Ryan and Lin's budding relationship. "I have to get back."

"Take these," Tamara says, handing me a warm bag of oatmeal chocolate chip cookies. "They'll make your snack mission look real."

Two stores away from the Knitorious, I pull my phone out of my pocket. With the bag of cookies in one hand, I use my free hand to text Adam.

Me: They found Fred at your new office. He's dead.

Eric looks up when the door jingles. He closes his notebook and clicks his pen closed. Ryan is carrying his toolbox toward the back room; it seems he's almost finished. I turn the sign from CLOSED to OPEN and offer Eric a cookie. He declines. Who says no to fresh-baked oatmeal chocolate chip cookies?

Ryan returns from the backroom and hands me the new keys and an invoice. I offer him a cookie, and he happily reaches into the bag. He says goodbye to Eric and me, and leaves through the back door. I follow him and lock the door behind him, being sure to lock the barrel-lock. Just in case.

Walking toward the front of the store, I sense Eric is waiting to get me alone and ask me more questions.

"Where were you on Friday night, Megan?"

I knew it.

I tell him about my girl's night with Connie and recommend the show we watched.

Does his question mean Fred's died on Friday night? Or was Friday night the last time anyone saw him? Today is Tuesday. We learned about Fred's disappearance on Sunday, so why is Eric asking me about Friday night?

"Where was Adam while you were having a girl's night?"

"I don't know." I shrug. "You'd have to ask Adam. I told you, we don't monitor each other's whereabouts anymore."

Where were you, Adam? I have a mental flashback to his lack of reaction when I told him Fred was missing.

"Why is Friday night important?" I ask.

"The coroner estimates Mr. Murphy's time of death was sometime between Friday night and Saturday morning. With any luck, he'll narrow it down when he conducts the autopsy today."

This is more information than I expect. Or than I'm used to Eric sharing.

"Did you find Fred today?" I ask, hoping Eric still feels talkative.

"Last night, a local resident reported someone abandoned a cube van outside 845 Mountain Road. The caller said they first noticed it early Saturday morning."

That doesn't quite answer my question but is still more information than I expected. I'm surprised news of another crime scene hasn't made its way all over town, and to the WSBA group chat by now. But this happened last night, after business hours. After most people on Mountain Road left their offices for the day.

Eric thanks me for my time. I offer him another cookie, which he declines because his willpower is obviously superhuman, and he leaves through the front door.

Adam hasn't responded to my text. I check again, and it says, *Read*, so I know he saw it. *Where are you, Adam? And where were you on Friday night?*

CHAPTER 28

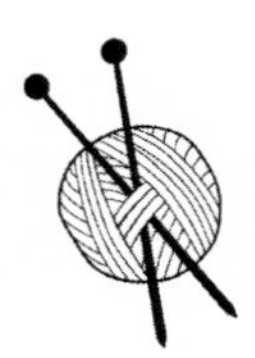

It's almost lunchtime when someone knocks at the back door. Good timing, my tummy is rumbling for lunch.

Connie has her overnight bag in one hand, and Harlow's kitty carrier in the other. Holding the door for her, I notice a box on the ground.

"That must be a delivery." Connie nods toward the box. "I wish they'd use the front door when no one answers back here. Maybe we should put up a sign."

I carry the box into the store and place it on the counter. It's heavier than I expect; whatever is inside this box isn't yarn. Yarn is light, and even large boxes don't weigh this much.

Connie releases Harlow from his carrier and leaves her overnight bag on the apartment stairs.

"Weird delivery," I comment to Connie. "There's no shipping label, no return address, nothing. Are we expecting anything from a local dyer? Maybe they dropped it off."

She shakes her head.

The sender sealed the box with tape and scrawled KNITORIOUS across the top in black marker. I grab the letter opener from the cup of pens beside the cash register and slice it open.

A rock. Odd. Who would send us a rock? And why? Upon closer inspection, this rock is familiar. Where have I seen it before? Connie peeks inside the box, but neither of us picks up the grey, heart-shaped rock.

Harlow rubs his head against the open flaps of the box and tries to jump inside. Connie scoops him up and cuddles him. He purrs but pulls away from her, toward the box. Connie takes him to the kitchenette and distracts him with kitty treats.

"Why would someone send us a rock?" Connie asks.

We're both a bit shaken by the strange delivery. I wrack my brain trying to remember where I've seen the rock before. It's on the tip of my brain, but just out of my mental reach. I move the box to the coffee table in the sitting area. Connie and I sit on the sofa and resume staring at it.

Connie asks me if I've heard about Fred's death—and it comes to me!

"This is the rock Kelly uses to keep the back door open at Hairway to Heaven!" I jump up and shout, like it's the winning answer on a TV game show.

Connie and I inspect the rock, being careful not to touch it. It's grey with streaks of darker grey, and on one edge, there are rust-coloured blotches.

"Connie, I think this might be blood," I say. "I don't remember these blotches on the rock the night Paul died."

Calm and focussed, Connie walks to the front door, locks it, turns the OPEN sign to CLOSED, picks up her phone, and calls Eric. Meanwhile, I take some photos of the rock and the box with my phone.

ERIC LOOKS at the rock and nods like this somehow makes sense to him.

"This is another murder weapon, isn't it?" I ask. "Was Fred murdered by chance? Maybe by a hit to the head?"

Instead of answering me, Eric asks questions.

He asks what time we noticed the box. I told him what time I opened the door for Connie.

The last person to use the door before Connie was Ryan.

No, there were no people or vehicles behind the store when Connie arrived.

No, I didn't hear anything. No one knocked at the door.

I give him a list of customers who visited Knitorious today.

No, the store doesn't have surveillance video.

No, we don't think Wilde Flowers has surveillance video either. In fact, we don't think any of the businesses on Water Street have surveillance video. Except maybe Charmed & Dangerous, the jeweler, but they're way up the street.

Eric asks a fellow officer to guard the rock and the box it arrived in.

He tells us they will dust the back door for prints, "just in case," then he goes outside and fetches crime scene tape from the trunk of his car parked in front of the store. He tapes off access to the parking lot so cars can't enter or leave. Then he tapes off the back door to stop anyone from touching it.

Connie and I watch Eric go next door to Wilde Flowers. Knitorious shares a driveway and parking lot with Wilde Flowers, so we presume he's asking Phillip if he noticed the box, or any people, or cars in the parking lot today.

Standing in the store with Connie and the box, I feel a shiver travel down my spine. Why would

Fred's killer bring the murder weapon here? Was the killer hoping I'd touch it and leave my fingerprints behind? Are they warning me I'm next? Is Fred's killer and Paul's killer the same person?

If there are two killers, it's unlikely both of them would send me evidence. Vulnerable and scared, I can't shake the feeling someone is watching me. Someone in my cozy, sweet town is murdering people and either trying to frame me for it or warn me that I'll be their next victim.

Connie suggests we close the store for the rest of the day. I agree with her idea, but I don't think we have a choice anyway, since it's a crime scene now.

Another uniformed officer opens the front door and greets the officer guarding the rock. He says he's here to pick up the box and the rock. Out of the corner of my eye, I spy Harlow gracefully and sneakily leap onto the table next to the box. I applaud his persistence. Connie sees him too, and when he launches himself again, she catches him mid-leap, preventing him from getting inside the box.

"I'll take Harlow upstairs, so he won't be in the way," I offer, holding out my hands to take the cat from her.

"Thank you, my dear." Connie smiles.

On my way upstairs, I pick up her overnight bag. I put Harlow and the bag in Connie's apartment and shut the door before he can bolt past me and run back to the store.

Part way down the stairs, I unlock my phone and sit for a moment.

Me: Are you finished questioning me? I'm not feeling well. I'd like to leave.

The low-grade nausea, which arrived at the exact moment I recognized the rock, is getting worse. I need to lie down. Somewhere quiet. Somewhere without a police presence.

Eric: I'll be there in a few minutes to drive you home.

It's a statement, not a question. He's not asking if I'd *like* him to drive me home, he's *informing* me he will drive me home. I suspect he wants to speak to Adam before I do.

Next, I text April and fill her in about the latest murder weapon showing up at Knitorious and send her the photos.

"Maybe I should stay," I suggest, struggling with guilt over leaving. "Or you could come home with me. It would give you a break from this." I gesture to the surrounding chaos.

"No need, my dear." Connie hugs me and rubs my back. "Archie is on his way here. You go home and get some rest." She tucks a stray curl behind my ear. "We'll talk in a couple of hours." She smiles.

Eric and I ride in silence to my house. Adam's car is in the driveway.

I drop my keys on the table by the door and march over to the dining room table, where Adam is doing whatever he does on his laptop.

"Why didn't you reply to my text?" I demand. "I know you saw it!" I'm almost shouting. Not quite, but close.

"Oh, jeez, Meg! I'm sorry," Adam says, smacking his forehead with his palm. "I saw it, but I was on the phone arranging insurance for the law practice. By the time I hung up, I forgot to text you back."

Really?! I tell him someone died, and it slips his mind to text me back?

When I tell Adam everything that happened today, the words explode out of me with such speed and urgency that Eric wouldn't be able to get a word in edgeways if he tried.

Then, after he's sufficiently overwhelmed with facts, I show Adam the photos of the rock I took with my phone.

Adam says nothing and focuses his gaze on the window while he processes the last few minutes.

"You took photos of the evidence?" Eric asks me while we wait for Adam to catch up.

I nod and show him the photos on my phone.

"Other than Connie and April, and now Adam, who else did you show them to?" he asks.

He's right, but I'm a little offended by his assumption.

"No one else," I say.

"Where were you on Friday night, Adam?" I ask.

I need to know, and Eric would've asked him, anyway.

"I was here until about 6 p.m., then I walked over to The Embassy for dinner," he recalls. "Friday's special is Fish and Chips. Halibut or haddock. I chose halibut. After dinner, I had a couple of pints, chatted with Sheamus about golf, and left after the Leaf's preseason game. I got home around 10 p.m.?" He snaps his fingers and looks at Eric. "Phillip saw me, he pulled into his driveway as I got to the front door. We said hello. He wanted to talk to me about the garden." Adam looks from Eric to me. "Phillip says you're an over-waterer, Meg."

Wracked with guilt for thinking—even for a minute—that Adam could kill Fred, I remind myself the Adam that I know isn't capable of murder. At least I don't think he is. I hope he's not.

Is he really incapable of murder, or do I *want to believe* he's incapable of murder? Now I'm second-guessing myself; I'm exhausted, defeated, and confused.

I flop onto the family room sofa with an exasperated sigh. The house is silent except for the low hum of voices from Eric and Adam talking in the dining room. A few minutes, or an hour later—I have no idea because my eyes are closed and I'm trying to relax by focussing on my breathing—Adam walks Eric to the door, and Eric leaves.

"Meg, I think it's time for us to lawyer-up."

"Of course, you do," I respond. "You're a lawyer, and lawyers always think that."

A lawyer will limit Eric's access to us, which would slow down the investigation. A lot.

"If you want to lawyer-up, go ahead," I tell him. "I'm not doing anything that might slow down the investigation. I have nothing to hide. I didn't do anything."

"Speaking of lawyers," Adam continues, "I have my annual golf retreat tomorrow with the guys from law school, remember? Well, I emailed them and cancelled. I don't feel comfortable being four hours away with all this going on. And I have a lot to do. The practice opens in three weeks."

Wait. What? I forgot about his golf retreat; I stopped putting Adam's events in my calendar weeks ago.

He needs to go. I need him to go. We've been together way too much since this investigation started. We need respite this two-night retreat will provide. I'd have the house to myself for two glorious nights!

"No!" I insist, waving my hands in front of me.

"Email them back and tell them you'll be there. You made these plans months ago, and we've already paid for it," I argue, trying to appeal to Adam's sense of practicality.

"I don't know…" he hems and haws.

Think, Megan, think! Give him all the reasons he should go.

"Listen, Adam, the last couple of weeks have been difficult. You left the firm, you were blackmailed twice, attended a funeral, and we've spent an uncomfortable amount of time together, which has been stressful. We're being investigated for murder, we're still adjusting to Hannah being away at school, and you're trying to set up a new practice in less than thirty days…" Gosh, it sounds awful when I say it out loud. "You deserve a couple of days away, to decompress, see your buddies, play some golf, and process everything that's happened." One last push; I put one hand on my chest and the other on his arm. "I think it would be unhealthy if you don't go," I whisper.

"I'll think about it," he says.

CHAPTER 29

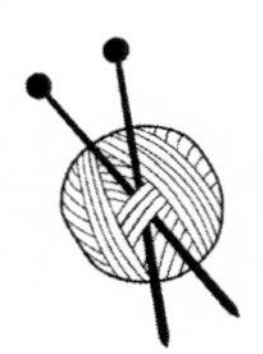

WEDNESDAY, September 25th

I sip my coffee and watch through the living room window as Adam loads his golf clubs into his car, relieved he's going to the golf retreat.

Before I leave, I put a bottle of pinot grigio in the fridge to chill. The thought of having the house to myself makes me giddy with excitement. My big plans include movies, wine, popcorn with extra butter, and finishing Hannah's cowl.

AT LUNCHTIME, Connie leaves for another mystery appointment, and it's just Harlow and me in the store for the rest of the afternoon.

I package online orders and chat with the local

charity knitting guild who visit the store on Wednesdays to knit, discuss future charity knitting projects, and order yarn for their upcoming projects. This month they're working on *knitted knockers* for the Knitted Knockers organization. Knitted knockers are prosthetic breast inserts that cancer survivors put in their bras after a mastectomy. They're always in demand at local hospitals and cancer support groups. Connie gives the charity guild a discount on the yarn they purchase for charity knitting.

The store closes at 6 p.m., but at 5:30 p.m., Harlow and I are the only ones here, so I close early and gather up the online orders, so I can drop them off before the post office closes.

After I give Harlow his dinner, I hide a few kitty treats in his favourite napping spots.

"Connie will be home soon," I assure the tuxedo cat as he cleans his face with his freshly licked paw.

AT THE POST OFFICE, I join the short line right behind Tamara who's mailing a care package to their daughter, Rachel. Tamara tells me she and April are going out for dinner and a movie tonight.

"You should join us," Tamara offers with a smile.

"Thanks," I respond, "but I've waited months to

have the house to myself, and I plan to enjoy every minute."

I also don't want to be the third wheel on their date night.

After Tamara drops off her package, we say goodbye on her way out, then I drop off the on-line orders and leave.

I have to walk back to Knitorious to get my car. Walking past Ho Lee Chow, my tummy rumbles, so I stop and peruse the menu in their window and contemplate adding a combo number seven to my evening plans.

"Hey Megan! It's nice to see you again. Your curly hair gave you away," the unfamiliar man says, walking toward me.

He's next to me now, and even up close I don't recognize him. How does he know my name? I'm sure we've never met.

"Hi!" I smile. "I'm sorry, have we met?"

"You don't remember me?" He clutches his chest and has a mock heart attack. "You're breaking my heart, Megan."

"I was your cab driver the other night," he reminds me, pointing to a taxi parked on the road.

The yellow car has Precious Cargo Cab Company painted on the side and printed on the roof light. I shake my head. He must have the wrong Megan.

"You flagged me down just off Mountain

Road?" he says, trying to jog my memory. "Really late Friday night... or I guess it was really early Saturday morning. You're even prettier in the daylight, by the way."

I still don't recognize him, but he piques my interest when he mentions Mountain Road and Friday night.

"You were at a house party and had a few drinks. You said you didn't want to drive home," he recalls. "You were walking home and flagged me down when I drove past. You don't remember any of it? Wow, you must've had more to drink than I thought."

"Where did you drop me off?" I ask.

"At home," he replies. "You live above the knitting store, right? I dropped you off out front."

I confirm he's referring to Knitorious, even though it's the only knitting store in town. He asks again if I live above it, but I don't answer him.

"I was kind of hoping we'd run into each other again," he says, shifting his weight and looking at the ground. "I was wondering if maybe I could get your number? We got along so well in the cab. But I'm not allowed to ask customers for their number. Since you're not in my cab, technically you're not a customer anymore." He shrugs with a smile.

I'm processing his words and twirling my ring.

"Is that a wedding ring?" He asks, pointing his chin toward my ring. "I looked for a ring when I drove you home. You weren't wearing one, so I assumed you're single. I'm sorry if I got it wrong."

"Was I wearing any other jewelry?" I ask.

"I don't think so." He shakes his head. "If you were, I didn't notice. Why? Did you lose something that night? I didn't find any jewelry when I cleaned out the cab after my shift. Sometimes there's an earring, or a broken necklace, or something, but nothing on Friday night." He pauses for a moment. "So, I guess getting your number is out of the question?"

I don't give him my number. Instead, I ask for his name and number, and he's eager to give me both. He's in a hurry to pick up an order from Ho Lee Chow and deliver it to a customer. Opening the door to the restaurant, he says he hopes to hear from me soon, then disappears inside.

He'll hear from someone soon, that's for sure.

I take a couple of photos of his cab with my phone, being sure to capture both the license plate number and the cab number.

I dial Eric's number and hurry toward Knitorious.

Voicemail.

"Hi, Eric. It's Megan Martel. Can you please call me back? It's important. Thanks." I end the call. "Where are you, Eric?" I mumble with a frustrated sigh.

I text him the photos of the cab, and the driver's

name and number. Then I send a second text with the highlights of my conversation with the cab driver, and what he said about our alleged interaction on Friday night.

I was neither at a house party, nor intoxicated when the driver said he picked me up on Mountain Road. In fact, I was nowhere near Mountain Road on Friday night, and I was never in a cab.

Unbeknownst to the driver, I wasn't in his cab on Friday night. Fred and Paul's killer was.

The knot in my stomach grows larger with every step I take toward Knitorious. Ignoring the pending sense of doom taking over my body, I pick up the pace as I close the distance between me and the parking lot. When my car is in sight, I sprint across the parking lot, pressing the button on the key chain that unlocks the door, and lock myself inside. I open my phone and plug it into the console, then stare at it.

Now what?

Should I call April? No. This investigation shouldn't upend her and Tamara's life, and I don't want to interrupt their date night. Between raising two kids, running a business, and the hectic pace of life, date nights for them are rare. I'm all too familiar with the consequences of ignoring the required maintenance of your marriage.

Should I call Connie? No. I'm not convinced she's being completely honest about her mystery appointments, and I don't want to cause her to worry or stress if it might impact her health.

Should I call Adam? What good would that do? He's four hours away from Harmony Lake. It's late in the day, so he's finished golfing and probably had at least a few drinks with his buddies by now.

Maybe I should call Kelly. No. Bad idea. If my suspicion is correct, calling Kelly could put one or both of us in danger. I cross this option off my mental list of potential next moves.

Why hasn't Eric called me back?

I take a few deep breaths and devise a plan. Go home, put on my pyjamas, then decide what to do. With any luck, in the meantime, Eric will call me back.

I lock the front door behind me, making sure I have my phone and didn't leave it in the car. Phone in hand, I take a deep breath, and drop my bag on the bench by the door. Looking forward to a chilled glass of pinot, I head toward the kitchen.

I gasp and bring my hand to my mouth.

My stomach sinks and my heart pounds double time.

"What are you doing here?" I demand. "How did you get in?"

CHAPTER 30

STEPHANIE MURPHY STARES at me from my kitchen table. She taps her leather-gloved finger on the handle of the gun laying on the table in front of her. Her curly hair is pulled into a tight bun,—I assume so she doesn't leave any stray hairs behind—and her expression is emotionless, her eyes empty, soulless voids.

I tighten my grip on my phone and move my hand behind my back.

"Hi Megan," Stephanie says, her voice flat. "I let myself in with the spare key. The one under the mat at the back door." She taps the table in front of her. "Put your phone here, please. I know it's in the hand behind your back."

I inch toward the table and Stephanie wraps her hand around the handle of the gun. Her index finger hovers over the trigger while I carefully place my phone on the table, face up. I take a few backward steps, never diverting my gaze from Stephanie and the gun.

"That's far enough," she says.

"How did you know about the spare key?" I ask.

"You're so predictably suburban, Megan," she chortles, rolling her eyes. "It was literally the second place I looked." she smiles, smug about her resourcefulness.

"What do you want?" I ask.

"To plant some evidence that will prove without a doubt it was you who killed Paul and Fred," she replies, "then kill you. Or more accurately, help you put yourself out of your misery."

"Adam will be back soon," I lie.

"Not according to the GPS tracker I put on his car." She shakes her head. Without breaking eye contact with me, Stephanie reaches into a pocket, retrieves her phone, and places it on the table in front of her. She grips the handle of the gun with one hand and uses her teeth to remove the glove from her other hand. She unlocks her phone. "He's over three hours away at a golf resort. We both know he won't be home tonight." She sneers.

Stephanie moves her hand away from the gun to put her glove back on, but she keeps the gun close to her. I don't have time to do anything, like run away or snatch the gun. I need to distract her while I think of a way out. I have to keep her talking.

"Where's Kelly?" I ask, inquiring about her sister. "Won't she wonder where you are?"

Please don't tell me you've hurt Kelly, or she's your partner in crime.

"Don't worry about Kelly," Stephanie replies. "She's sound asleep until tomorrow morning. I'm getting better at dosing the sleeping medication. Her deep sleep should last long enough that she won't notice my absence, and she won't wake up groggy and suspicious."

"You drug your sister?"

"Only sometimes." She shrugs like it's no big deal. "Like tonight, so I can visit you. And Friday night when I snuck out to... take care of Fred. Other than that, just here and there. It helps her sleep without waking up in the night, crying over her loser husband." Stephanie shakes her head. "What a waste of tears," she scoffs.

It's safe to assume Stephanie hated Paul.

"I also drugged Fred the night I visited Paul," she adds. "And tonight, I'm going to drug you, except you won't wake up." She smiles.

She's a psychopath. I have to get out of here.

"Your phone will give you away," I say. "If the police check it, they'll know you were here. If you leave now, I won't say anything. If anyone asks, I'll say you picked up something for Kelly."

I know she won't fall for it, but I need to prolong this conversation as long as possible while I plan my escape.

"It's a burner," she informs me. "I'll dispose of it as soon as I leave."

Of course, it is and of course, she will. She's thought of everything.

"How? Like down a sewer grate, or something?" I ask, stalling what feels like my inevitable downfall.

Ding!

Before Stephanie can answer me, my phone dings and we both look at the screen. It's a text.

Eric: Call me.

By instinct, I take a step forward. Stephanie points the gun at me, shaking her head.

Brrrrring! Brrrrring! My phone lights up. Eric's name flashes on the call display, and I've never wanted to answer a phone call so much in my life.

Still pointing the gun at me, Stephanie uses her other gloved hand to turn off the phone. "I understand why you killed Paul," I say, trying to sound sympathetic. "He stole the photos you sent to Kelly and used them to blackmail people. He would've exposed your affair with Adam. But why did you kill Fred? He's your husband, and he loved you. He told me at Paul's celebration of life."

"You've got some things right," Stephanie admits. "I didn't want my affair with Adam to become public knowledge, and Paul stealing the photos from Kelly was the final straw. But the biggest reason was to save my sister. Paul was a loser, and he sucked her dry financially again and again. Yet, despite everything he'd done, Kelly insisted she loved him, and refused to leave him. He would've kept dragging her down with him. Paul knew she was too good for him, that's why he spied on her phone and her email. He knew she'd realize she could do better and leave him."

"So, you went to see Paul that night intending to kill him?" I clarify.

Committing murder with yarn and a knitting needle she found at the crime scene, before sunset, with witnesses right downstairs, doesn't seem well planned. And judging by the predicament I find myself in, Stephanie strikes me as a meticulous planner.

"No. I never planned to kill anyone," she explains. "When he discovered my affair with Adam, Fred and I agreed there could be no more secrets. We agreed to be honest with each other to save our marriage. That's when Fred told me he loaned Paul money. He helped Paul pay off his latest gambling debt and stop a money lender from placing a lien on the building. If they lost the building, my sister would have lost her home and business." The tone of Stephanie's voice grows angrier as she speaks, and her jaw clenches tighter until she's speaking through her clenched teeth. "I was furious. To make it worse, Fred told me Paul planned to pay us back by robbing my sister's business and selling her equipment. Fred said Paul already had a buyer lined up. He said Kelly wouldn't lose any money because she had insurance." She shakes her head and tears well up in her eyes.

At least, I think tears are welling up in her eyes. It's hard to tell for sure. The sun is setting, and inside the house is getting darker by the minute.

"Fred seemed OK with this robbery scheme, which made me more furious," she continues. "So, after an early dinner, I helped Fred fall asleep. Then, I left my phone at home and drove to Harmony Lake. My plan was to tell my sister about Paul's latest gambling debt, Fred's loan to stop the foreclosure of the building, and her husband's plan to steal from her."

Tears stream down Stephanie's cheeks. While she pauses for a few breaths and composes herself, I wonder why she left her phone at home if she wasn't planning to kill Paul.

"Would you like a glass of water?" I ask, in part to buy time, and in part to keep her calm since she has a gun.

Maybe I can throw the glass at her head and run away. She shakes her head.

"The back door was open. Kelly used a rock to

prop it open and let in some fresh air," Stephanie recalls. "I went inside, but Kelly was busy with a customer and didn't notice me. I didn't want to interrupt, so I went upstairs to the apartment. It never occurred to me Paul would be there. He's part of so many committees, and organizations that Kelly says he's out almost every evening. But when I opened the door, there he was, standing in the kitchen in his undershirt, pouring milk into a giant bowl of cereal. I felt sick just looking at him. I confronted him. I told him I knew about the gambling, the money lender, and the robbery plan. He was so smug and arrogant."

Our eyes are locked, but in my peripheral vision, through the window behind her, the bushes rustle. Like a large animal is there. The largest animal I've ever seen in the backyard is an obese squirrel who eats scraps the neighbours leave him. I blink, attempting to reset my vision in case my eyes are playing tricks on me.

"He held up his phone and showed me the photos," Stephanie recollects, holding up her empty hand as if she were holding a phone. "He admitted he stole them from Kelly's phone. Paul threatened me. He said if I told Kelly, he'd send them to every lawyer and every law firm in the country. He demanded twenty thousand dollars to keep quiet and gave me until midnight to transfer the money to his account. Then he told me to leave, or he'd upload the photos to social media sites that instant. He turned the TV on and sat at the table to eat his cereal."

Stephanie talks like she's in a trance. Her face is emotionless, and her tone of voice is eerily calm and even. She's looking into my eyes, but I'm not sure if she sees me, or the events she's reliving. Her steady hand rests on the gun.

"I left," she says, "but part way down the stairs, I realized I could have Paul charged with extortion and harassment. I decided to threaten him and beat him at his own game. So, I went back to the apartment. The TV was blaring, and he didn't hear me come in. He was at the table, sitting with his back to me. He slurped his cereal so loudly I heard it over the TV. This was my opportunity. I could rid myself, and my sister, of him forever. Eliminate him. The yarn and knitting needles were right in front of me. The yarn was already in a big loop. I wrapped it around my hands and put one of the knitting needles in my mouth. Then I crept up behind him, looped the yarn around his neck, and pulled with all my might. I couldn't get it tight enough. I wasn't strong enough. Using the knitting needle as a garrote, I tightened the yarn around his neck. Paul kicked his feet and tried to pry his fingers between the yarn and his neck. Then he just stopped. I let go of the yarn slowly, and his head fell forward into the cereal bowl. He looked dead, but I wasn't sure. I hoped he was dead, but I didn't want to check. I crept backwards out of the apartment. I kept the knitting needle in case Paul woke up. If he attacked me, I could stab him with it or something."

Stephanie blinks a few times and rejoins me in the present moment. She dabs her eyes with a gloved finger.

"When you think about it, I did you and Adam a favour by killing Paul," she proclaims. "If he made those photos public, it would have ruined all of our lives."

I hope she doesn't expect me to thank her.

Stephanie pulls a pill bottle from the pocket of her jacket and places it on the table next to the gun and my phone.

"I could use a glass of wine," I state, ignoring the pill bottle. "Would you like some?"

I don't want wine; I want the bottle. Maybe if I hurl it at Stephanie's head, I can separate her from the gun long enough to escape.

"No thank you," she replies. "But you go ahead. You'll need something to swallow these with,"—she smiles and shakes the pill bottle—"and wine will get the job done."

Making slow, intentional movements so Stephanie won't panic and shoot me, I open the cupboard and get a wine glass. A shard of glass could be a good back-up weapon if my wine bottle idea doesn't work. I inhale and swallow hard, nervous about turning my back on Stephanie long enough to retrieve the wine bottle from the fridge.

"Why did you kill Fred?" I ask, trying to distract her. "Because he found out you killed Paul?"

"No," she replies. "He believed either you or Adam murdered Paul."

As she speaks, I open the fridge and get the wine, then turn to face her again, closing the fridge door with my hip.

"After he died, we found out Paul had no insurance," Stephanie says. "My sister couldn't afford his final expenses, so Fred and I paid for everything. Fred resented spending the money. He wanted to get some of it back by following through with Paul's plan to burglarize the salon. I begged him not to do it. I told him if he got caught, he'd go to jail. Fred relented and promised me he wouldn't rob the salon. Then, on Friday night, Fred said he was going to work for a few hours because something came up.

I open the bottle and leave it on the counter to breathe while I choose my moment.

"He lied," she continues to unburden herself. "According to the GPS tracker I put on Fred's car, he didn't go to work. He went to a truck rental place. I knew right away what he was doing, and I drove to the salon. The rental truck was parked by the back door. I tried to reason with him. I begged him not to do it. He told me everything was my fault. He said if I hadn't had an affair, then you and Adam wouldn't have killed Paul to keep it a secret, and Paul wouldn't have died before he could pay us back."

It's an excellent theory, but Fred couldn't have been more wrong. I pour some wine into the glass.

"He turned his back to me to open the back of the truck. I picked up the rock by the salon door and hit him in the head," Stephanie confesses. "The top of his body fell into the open truck, I just had to lift his bottom half up there too. I locked him in the back of the truck and thought about what to do next. I needed to point the evidence toward you and Adam. I looked at Adam's GPS and saw that he'd spent time at 845 Mountain Road, so that's where I left Fred and the truck. After I dropped off Fred, I hailed a passing cab and pretended I was you. It was late, and I was too tired to walk back to Water Street. I asked the cab driver to drop me off at Knitorious. From there, I walked to the salon to collect my car and the rock."

"The cab driver fell for it," I confirm, picking up the wine glass and swirling the contents while I work up the nerve to put my plan into action.

"I told the driver my name was Megan," Stephanie admits. "It was dark, we have similar hair, and similar body types, so I figured if the police asked the cab driver who was in his cab, he'd lead them to you." She shrugs a shoulder.

Now or never. I bring the glass to my lips and take a small sip. When returning the glass to the counter, I miss on purpose, and it shatters on the wood floor.

"Darn it!" I yell, jumping back when the wine glass hits the floor.

Stephanie grabs the gun and stands up to assess the situation. Shards of glass and splattered wine cover the kitchen floor. She isn't reacting as I hoped she would. I hoped the breaking glass would startle Stephanie enough to jump up *without* grabbing the gun. Her eyes dart back and forth from me to the mess on the floor.

"I better pick these up." Eying the biggest, sharpest shard of glass, I bend to pick it up.

"Stop!" Stephanie shouts. "Don't move!" She cocks the gun.

"OK, transcription stopped," says Oscar's humanoid voice as I raise my hands to my shoulders and slowly stand up.

I guess Adam didn't uninstall the glitchy dictation app before he left.

Stephanie looks in the direction Oscar's voice came from, then back at me. Her eyes are wide with panic and confusion.

"Who said that? What does it mean?" She's raises the gun higher, aiming it at my head.

I tell her about Oscar and explain the dictation app that Adam installed.

"You know how much Adam loves technology," I quip, trying to de-escalate her stress level. I stare down the barrel of the gun she's still pointing at my head. "He has to try every new gadget." I shrug. "He just can't help himself."

I explain that this specific app has a glitch and sometimes records when it's not supposed to.

"How do we erase it?" She demands with urgency.

"We don't," I reply. "The device emails the transcript to Adam. It's probably in his inbox already."

Stephanie's eyes are wide with horror, and her hand trembles, making the gun unsteady. I mentally ask the universe to please make her scared enough to make a mistake, but not scared enough to shoot me.

"Go get it and bring it here," Stephanie demands, waving the gun between me and Oscar.

With my hands still raised, I take slow steps to the end table in the family room, sensing the gun as it follows my every step. This positions me close to the front door. I could be outside in three seconds. I squat slowly, turning my head toward Stephanie. I explain to her that I have to lower my hands to move the table and unplug the device.

I have no intention of unplugging anything. I have a new plan.

Stephanie nods and I turn my attention back to Oscar. Out of the corner of my eye, an indistinct blur moves near the front door. I blink, looking into the darkness, but there's nothing. The stress of this situation must be messing with me.

I lower my hands and pretend to reach behind the table, but I pick up the ceramic yarn bowl instead. With my back still to Stephanie, I stand up, holding the yarn bowl against my chest like a Frisbee.

In one fast motion, I spin toward Stephanie and launch the yarn bowl, frisbee-style, toward her head. As the ceramic sheep-inspired bowl hurtles through the air, Stephanie instinctively raises her hands and turns her head to protect her face, pointing the gun toward the ceiling.

I run.

"Oscar! Unlock the door," I shout.

"OK," Oscar replies as the lock clicks.

Reaching for the doorknob, something behind me shuffles, and without looking, I imagine Stephanie coming after me. As I turn the doorknob, the door swings open, forcing me behind it, into a corner. Police rush through the open door. I try to weave through the onslaught of blue uniforms and escape. One of them grabs my waist and shoves me into the corner. He stands, gun drawn, with his back to me like a human shield.

Bang! A single gunshot.

A thud.

Stephanie lets out a breathy grunt.

I crouch down to make myself the smallest target possible and try to peek around and through the officer's legs.

I can't see anything except a gun on the family room floor. My human shield adjusts his stance, and Stephanie's top half comes into view. She's facedown with a knee wedged in her back. Someone cuffs her hands behind her back. The cop on her back leans forward. It's Eric.

"He's hit!" a woman's voice yells.

He who? Who's hit? Did Stephanie shoot Eric?

"Who's hit?" I ask my human shield.

No answer. Either he can't hear me or he's ignoring me. I ask louder. No answer.

The house is crawling with police officers, inside and out. The lights from the patrol cars bounce off the walls, creating a strobe effect. One by one, the police turn on every light in the house.

"All clear!" the woman's voice yells.

The human shield turns to me and takes my arm.

"Are you OK?" he asks, pulling me up from my crouched position.

I nod as he looks me over, checking for signs of injury.

Physically, I'm OK. Aside from that, I'm not sure yet, stay tuned.

Still kneeling next to Stephanie, Eric stands up and walks toward me, smiling.

"Were you shot?" I scan him for evidence of a gunshot wound.

"No," he says, shaking his head and smiling.

How can he smile? He smiles in the face of murder, turns down fresh oatmeal chocolate chip cookies, Eric Sloane is a freak. A freak who just saved my life.

"I heard a gunshot," I insist. "Someone said, *he's hit*."

"She was talking about Oscar," Eric explains. "Stephanie shot Oscar. He was the only casualty tonight. Well, Oscar and your yarn bowl."

"Poor Oscar," I say.

I'll miss him.

ERIC GOT the photos of the cab and the information about the driver I texted to him earlier. When I didn't answer his text or phone call, he knew there was a problem. He came to the house, peeked in a few windows, and assessed the situation. Then he contacted Adam, who used the app on his phone to unlock the house. Back-up arrived without lights and sirens, and officers surrounded the house, positioning themselves so Stephanie wouldn't see them if she looked outside. This explains why the bushes in the backyard were moving; it wasn't my eyes after all.

Eric sneaked into the house and hid. He aimed his gun at Stephanie and waited. Biding his time until she pointed her gun away from me and he could intervene. He was the blur I saw near the front door before I attempted to escape. He heard her entire confession.

When I flung the yarn bowl at Stephanie's head, it gave Eric the opportunity to sneak up behind her while I was out of the line of fire. That was the shuffling, gunshot, thud, and grunt I heard. Eric says he lunged at her and grabbed her wrists, commandeering her arms to keep her from aiming the gun at anyone. Stephanie put up a struggle, and the gun discharged, shooting Oscar. Stephanie hit the floor face first with Eric on her back. Oscar was in the wrong place at the wrong time.

CHAPTER 31

Wednesday, October 2nd

April and I took a road trip to Toronto for a few days to visit Hannah and Rachel. We took the girls shopping and saw a musical. On our way home, we stopped for two days of pampering and spa treatments at Ste. Anne's Spa. The break and change of scenery gave me the time and space I needed to process everything that happened.

When I got home last night, I found boxes scattered throughout the house. Moving boxes. Adam is moving! He's moving into one of the new condos at the Harbourview Condominium complex. He gets possession this weekend and says he'll move on Saturday, if I'm ready to be alone in the house. I am. More than ready.

Besides, while I was away, he had a state-of-the-art security system installed, complete with cameras. I live in the safest house in Harmony Lake.

Today is my morning off, but I work this afternoon. I take my time walking to work and stop at Latte Da. I've missed their coffee.

Standing in the long line, I'm deciding what to order, when someone taps my shoulder.

"I saw you walk past the salon and took a chance that you would stop for coffee," Kelly says hesitantly.

I throw my arms around her. She hugs me tightly and we cry. Ugly crying. Sobbing. The loud, wet, messy crying that isn't discreet. We help ourselves to napkins and find a quiet corner. We start speaking at the same time, apologizing to each other.

She's sorry for not realizing her sister was a psychopath. I'm sorry she lost her husband and brother-in-law. She's sorry she didn't tell me her sister was having an affair with Adam as soon as she found out. I'm sorry I suspected her of murder. She's sorry she hasn't called since Stephanie almost killed me. I'm sorry I didn't call her to warn her when I figured out Stephanie was the killer. When we run out of tears and apologies, we get back in line to order our coffees.

"Eric let me see Stephanie," Kelly whispers

while we wait for our coffees. "I asked her not to cause any more suffering with a trial. She agreed."

"It's over?" I ask, dubious. "Like, completely over?"

"It's over," she assures me, nodding.

We get our coffees and go outside. After another long hug, we agree to meet at Ho Lee Chow for dinner after work. Kelly returns to the salon, and I continue to Knitorious.

The jingle of the bell above the door, and the warm, comforting smell of the store hit me and I realize how much I missed the store. I close the door behind me and stand still, taking deep breaths and allowing the comfort to wash over me and through me.

"Welcome back, my dear." Connie gives me a long, swaying hug. "The store isn't the same without you," she says when we finally pull apart.

"Welcome back, Megan," Archie says, hugging me. "Thank goodness you're OK," he whispers in my ear.

We sit in the cozy sitting area, and Harlow wakes up from his nap in the front window. He gives me the side-eye, indulges in a yawn accompanied by a long stretch, then slinks over. Purring, he graces my lap with his presence.

Connie and Archie ask after Hannah and Rachel, so I pull out my phone and show them photos of our visit while Connie fusses over me and strokes my hair.

I tell them about Adam moving out, but they already know. Apparently, I'm the last one to find out.

"We look forward to having him as a neighbour," Connie says, then exchanges a sneaky glance with Archie.

"I don't follow," I say.

"Well, my dear, Archie and I also purchased one of the new condos," Connie explains. "It's time we take our relationship to the next level. I was going to move to Archie's house"—she gestures to Archie —"but Ryan lives there, too, and he wouldn't want to live with two senior citizens."

"And I'd love to move here," Archie adds, "but the stairs to the apartment are too much for my hip." He gyrates his hips to illustrate his point.

"So, we decided a new condo would be perfect," Connie concludes. "It's not his, it's not mine, it's ours." She has that content, optimistic glow that people get when they're in love.

"And it's perfect for the 'retirement lifestyle' we're trying out," Archie says, using air quotes around "retirement lifestyle."

Wow. A lot can happen in a week.

"I'm happy for you," I say. "It's wonderful news. So, does this explain your mystery appointments? You were house hunting?"

"Yes!" Connie taps my knee. "And I'm so glad it's over. If I never shop for another home again, it'll be too soon."

"I assume Harlow will move to the condo too? Or will he make the daily commute?" I ask.

Connie and Archie laugh.

"He's coming with us," she confirms. "But we're planning to do some travelling, and we'd like him to stay at Knitorious while we're away. If that's OK with you, my dear."

Of course, it's OK with me! Harlow belongs here. He's as much a part of Knitorious as Connie and the yarn.

"Who will run Knitorious while you two globe trot and try out your 'retirement lifestyle?'" I ask, using air quotes for the first time in my life.

"You will, of course," Connie replies, like it's the most obvious thing in the world. "Knitorious needs you, and you need Knitorious. I'm not the only one entering a new phase of life. You aren't a wife and full-time mother anymore, my dear. You're a soon-to-be-single woman who has a grown child and a business to run."

"You want me to work full-time?" I ask, confused.

"I want you to *own* it, my dear," Connie clarifies. "We'll work out the details later, but trust me, you need this store, and this store needs you. I knew when I met you almost seventeen years ago that you would take over Knitorious one day."

For the second time today, tears fill my eyes, and a lump forms in my throat. I blink back tears and try to swallow the lump while Connie takes my hand, and Archie gets the box of tissues from the counter.

"I'll still be here part time, when we aren't travelling," Connie explains, waggling her index finger. "You'll never get rid of me, no matter how hard you try." She winks. "But it's time for me to step aside and watch you blossom. It's time for you to make this store your own."

I don't know what to say, and I'm too choked up to talk, anyway. With tears streaming down my face, I nod and reach out to hug her, squishing Harlow.

When the bell above the door jingles, Connie gets up and greets Eric while I dry my eyes and compose myself. She and Archie tell him about their new condo.

Why does it seem like every time I see Eric, I've either just finished crying, or I'm on the verge of crying? He must think I'm an emotionally unstable mess. I stand up and turn around to face them.

"Hi Eric," I say smiling.

He didn't get any less hot while I was away. In fact, he's hotter than I remember.

"Hi Megan." He smiles. "Welcome home. Don't worry, I'm not here to question you." He chuckles.

I laugh with him, thinking this is the first time he's shared his sense of humour. Solving this case agrees with him; this is the most relaxed I've ever seen him.

"I'm returning the items we took into evidence. The huge purse and its contents." He hands me a gift bag and a large evidence bag filled with smaller evidence bags. "Except the knitting needle," he adds. "We have to keep that."

He can keep the knitting needle forever, for all I care. I never want to see it again. I put the evidence bag behind the counter and open the gift bag, and pull out a heavy wad of tissue paper.

"A small token of my appreciation for your help with this case," Eric explains. "I know it's not the same as the one you made," he says, switching his weight from one foot to the other, "but I wanted to replace the one you lost. Connie gave me the number of a local potter who makes them."

I open the tissue paper and find a new sheep-shaped yarn bowl. Similar to the one that broke when I hurled it at Stephanie's head.

"Thank you," I say. "I love it. It's one of the most thoughtful gifts I've ever received. Actually, I have something for you too."

I reach into my caramel-coloured tote, pull out a gift bag, and hand it to him.

"I was going to drop it off at the station later. To say thank you for saving my life, and my reputation, and believing I was innocent."

He opens the bag and pulls out the hat and scarf I knitted for him. I found the yarn at Romni Wools when April and I were in Toronto. I knit them in the car, when it was April's turn to drive, and at the spa. It's a worsted-weight, merino blend in the same shade of forest green as the polo shirt he wore the night we had dinner at the store and he questioned me. The yarn has honey-coloured flecks of tweed that match the honey-coloured flecks in his eyes.

He saved my life; it's the least I could do. No gift will ever be adequate to thank him.

Either Eric Sloane is a talented actor, has good manners, or he's touched by the gift.

"Thank you. I love them." He clears his throat. "No one has ever knit for me."

"Really? Well, I knit a small gift of appreciation for everyone who saves my life," I tease. "So, there could be more hand-knit gifts in your future if you save my life again."

He laughs. "I'll keep that in mind."

"So, what's next for you?" I ask. "I'm sure you're ready to wave goodbye to our quirky little town and watch us fade in your rear-view mirror as you move on to bigger and better cases."

"Funny you should ask," Eric responds.

"Harmony Lake PD is starting their own major crimes unit, and they offered me a position."

"And?" I ask. "What did you say?"

"I hope they offered to make you the head of the department," Connie adds.

"I accepted," he answers me, then looks at Connie. "And yes, I will be in charge of the unit. The unit of one. Me. I will be the major crimes division of the HLPD."

We congratulate him, and Archie shakes his hand.

"This town is perfect for me," Eric says. "I can fish in the summer and ski in the winter. And with the low crime rate, I'll have enough time off to enjoy both."

I guess I'll be seeing him around town since he'll be a local.

He asks if we can recommend a real estate agent since he'll need somewhere to live in town. Connie asks him what he's looking for in a home, and he lists his criteria: something small, no yard to maintain, and centrally located. He says he doesn't have very much stuff but needs enough room to store his fishing gear, ski equipment, and a jet ski.

Connie looks at me. I look back at her and smile. She widens her eyes and upgrades her look to a glare, and I sense I'm missing something. She opens her eyes even wider and nods her head. She's trying to tell me something, I just know it. But I'm not getting it. I'm better at this game when April and I play it.

Giving up, Connie lets out an exasperated sigh, and throws her hands in the air.

"It just so happens, Detective Sergeant, that I'll be moving out of the upstairs apartment in the next few weeks, and it will be vacant," Connie says.

"Would you consider renting it to me?" Eric asks. "It would be perfect!"

"That would be up to the owner," Connie replies, glaring at me.

I smile, sure I'm missing something again.

"Megan, will you be looking for a tenant for the upstairs apartment?" she asks.

It's me! I'm the owner, I realize, catching up to everyone else in this conversation. The idea of owning Knitorious is so new, I haven't grasped it yet.

"Yes! I'd love to have you upstairs," I declare.

An immediate rush of heat floods my face as the last word leaves my mouth, and I realize how it sounds. I'm sure Eric knows what I mean. Talking to him as a cop is easier than talking to him as a... friend? Potential tenant? Neighbour?

Harlow winds himself around Eric's ankles. *Thank you, Harlow, for the distraction.*

"Harlow obviously wants you to move in, and I can't say no to him," I say.

"You've never seen the upstairs apartment, have

you Eric?" Connie asks. "Megan, why don't you take Eric upstairs so he can see what he's agreeing to before he commits."

"Sure!" I look at Eric. "Do you have a few minutes?"

"Lead the way," he says.

As we climb the stairs, Eric says, "I didn't realize you own Knitorious. I thought Connie was the owner."

"Ditto," I say, opening the apartment door and stepping inside. "I only found today that I'll be the owner," I explain. "I'm still getting used to the idea. There's been a lot of change lately, you know? Hannah moved away, my marriage ended, I was a murder suspect, then almost a murder victim, and now I'm about to become a business owner. It's a lot to keep up with."

"You'll be an amazing business owner," he says, looking into my eyes. "And landlady." He walks around, giving himself a tour of the apartment. "This place is perfect! I love it!"

"Then it's yours!" I tell him. "You can move in as soon as Connie moves out. Listen Eric, thank you again for saving my life. I'm not sure it would've ended well if you hadn't shown up when you did."

"Yes, it would," he assures me, nodding. "You're smarter and tougher than you give yourself credit for." He walks into a bedroom and raises his voice so I can hear him, "I think you have it backwards. I might have saved Stephanie from you." He comes back into the kitchen. "You were practically out of there when I intervened. You would've fought your way out, and you would've won, whether any cops showed up. Trust me, I have good instincts about these things." He smiles. "And please stop thanking me now."

"Just one more." I hold up my index finger. "Thank you for putting up with me nosing around in your investigation. I'm sure I didn't make your job any easier."

"You were a huge help," he insists. "You'd make a great partner."

"That was it," I say, "The last thank you. Well for this. If you do something else nice for me, I reserve the right to thank you for it."

"Deal," he agrees, extending his hand, and we shake on it.

"Harmony Lake isn't usually this exciting, you know," I warn him. "If you're expecting a steady flow of murder investigations, it might disappoint you when you realize the major crimes unit solves cases like littering, jaywalking, and double parking. Maybe you should sign a short-term lease in case you miss the excitement of the big city."

"I have a feeling Harmony Lake is more exciting than it looks." He smirks. "And if it isn't, that's fine with me. I'm ready for a bit of boredom. It'll be a nice change.

We laugh and head back downstairs.

TURN the page for a sneak peek of Killer Cables: A Knitorious Murder Mystery Book 2

KILLER CABLES

CHAPTER 1

TUESDAY JANUARY 7TH

"Who's a smart girl? It's you! That's right, you're a smart girl!" I say with a high-pitched and excited voice.

I squeeze the plush duckie to make it quack and toss it across the room.

"Go get it Sophie!"

Sophie scurries across the wood floor and down the hall. She doesn't apply her corgi-brakes fast enough and slides past the duckie and into the carpet by the front door. She shakes it off, picks up the duckie and prances back to me proudly with her head held high.

Sophie has been staying with me since last week when her human, Laura Pingle, slipped on a patch of ice while taking her trash to the curb and broke her leg in two places. Laura was rushed to the hospital, had to have emergency surgery, and I jumped at the opportunity to look after Sophie until she gets home.

"Which sweater do you want to wear today, Sophie?"

Laura is a knitter, so Sophie has an impressive wardrobe of hand-knit dog sweaters. I grabbed about eight of them when I picked up Sophie's supplies at Laura's house and I left behind at least eight more. Most of them have some shade of purple as either the main colour or an accent colour.

"How about this one?" I ask, holding up her purple and black hounds tooth sweater with a folded turtleneck.

She doesn't disagree (she never does, she's an easy going roommate), so I slip the sweater over her head. By instinct, she lifts one paw, then the other so I can feed them through the impossibly short sleeves of the sweater; she's done this before and knows the drill.

I attach her purple leash to her purple collar, slip on my winter boots, crush my curly, chestnut-brown hair under a hand-knit hat, wrap the matching scarf around my neck, put on my coat, and zip it up.

I check my pockets to make sure my gloves are there, check Sophie's leash to make sure we have enough poop bags for the day and grab my cranberry-coloured tote bag.

One last look in the mirror by the door; I remove a stray eyelash from under one of my hazel eyes, pull my lip balm from my purse and smear a layer on my lips to act as a barrier against the cold, dry, winter air.

"Oscar, I'm leaving," I say into the void.

"OK. I'm arming the house," Oscar replies in a humanoid voice.

Oscar is a digital voice assistant. This is my second Oscar. My ex-husband, Adam, and our eighteen-year-old daughter, Hannah, gave him to me for Christmas.

I call him Oscar 2.0. because Oscar 1.0 died suddenly last September when he was shot by a killer who broke into my house to kill me. Thankfully, Oscar 1.0 was the only fatality that night. The killer's previous two victims weren't as lucky; they lost their lives, I only lost a WI-FI enabled device.

Sophie and I leave the house and I hear the door lock behind me. Good job, Oscar.

I started the car ten minutes ago using the remote starter on my keychain. It's too cold to walk to Water Street, so Sophie and I get in the warm car for the short drive to work.

I PARK in the small parking lot behind the store, and instead of going in through the back door like I would normally, Sophie and I walk around to the front of the store and across the street to the park so Sophie can have a walk and do her business.

This time of year, this early in the day, and this close to the lake, it's too cold to stay outside for very long, so this isn't a leisurely stroll, it's a business call, and as soon as Sophie finishes we high-tail it back across the street to Knitorious.

I unlock the front door and kick the snow off my boots against the brick wall next to it. Then I turn the knob and open the door, listening for the jingle of the bell, one of my favourite sounds.

Knitorious is warm and cozy and feels like home. Other than my house, it's the only place where walking through the door makes me feel both relaxed and reinvigorated at the same time.

I undo Sophie's leash and take her sweater off. She gives herself a shake, and follows me to the back room where I put our outerwear and her leash away. I freshen Sophie's water bowl, turn on the lights in the store, unlock the front door, and flip the sign from closed to open.

"It's showtime," I say to Sophie, just like Connie always says to me when she unlocks the door and turns the sign.

Tuesdays aren't our busiest day of the week, but

we're in the midst of the winter tourist season, so I expect a steady flow of customers.

Despite Harmony Lake's small size, we squeeze in a large population of tourists during the winter and summer tourist seasons.

In the winter, tourists flock to the two ski resorts in the Harmony Hills Mountains, various rental houses, and the new condominium development at the end of Water Street, and in the summer, they flock to the same places for access to the lake and the small-town-living experience.

Besides being small, Harmony Hills is secluded which gives it the feeling of being further away from the hustle and bustle of the city than it is.

I can see the lake from the front window of the store, across the street, just beyond the park where I walked Sophie. Behind me, to the north, are the Harmony Hills Mountains. Tiny, as far as mountain ranges go, but a popular destination for weekend skiers and snowboarders. Geographically, Harmony Lake can't be a bigger town. Not without moving either a lake or a small mountain range.

Knitorious is closed on Sundays and Mondays, so I spend Tuesdays returning phone calls and emails and processing online orders that were placed on the store website over the weekend. I turn on the laptop and, while waiting for it to power up, check the store voicemail.

The bell over the door jingles, and a well-wrapped Connie comes in from the cold.

"Good morning, Megan, my dear."

She always says it in a sing-song voice.

Sophie jumps up from her dog bed to greet Connie and is wagging her Corgi butt while she follows Connie to the back room.

"Good morning to you, too, Sophie," Connie sings from the back room.

Connie is my mother-friend, and I'm her daughter-friend.

We met sixteen years ago when Adam, Hannah, and I first moved to Harmony Lake. We became instant friends and soon after we became family.

I lost my mum just after Hannah's first birthday, and Hannah was born when I was barely twenty-one, so when Connie and I met, I was young, newly married, a new mum, and grieving. She welcomed us, nurtured us and filled the mother and grandmother-shaped holes we had in our hearts. At almost seventy years young, she's the most beautiful, smart, and sophisticated woman I know.

I started working here part-time about five years ago and became the store owner a few months ago when Connie decided it was time for her to retire and move out of the upstairs apartment. She moved into a new condo with her boyfriend, Archie, and I took over as owner of Knitorious. So, now I own

Knitorious and Connie works here part time. We've come full circle.

"Today feels bittersweet," Connie says as she crouches down to pet Sophie.

"I know. It'll be hard to let her go," I say, "It's been nice having a pet in the store again, and we fit together so well, you know? We're like kindred spirits. At home, we both like to eat, we both like to nap, and we both like to cuddle. At the store, we both like to greet the customers and visit with everyone. I'll miss her."

"Well, Archie and I are going south in a couple of weeks, so you'll have Harlow to help you run the store and keep you company while we're away. I know Laura has missed Sophie dearly and can't wait to see her."

Harlow is Connie's cat. When Connie owned the store and lived upstairs, Harlow had unrestricted access to both the store and the apartment. He was a fixture here. Even non-knitters would come in just to visit him. The store feels incomplete without him here, but I get custody of him when Connie and Archie travel, so he stays at Knitorious while they're away.

"Phillip said he's picking Laura up from the hospital and taking her home this morning. Once she's settled, I'll take Sophie home to her, "I explain. "According to Phillip, Laura's looking at six weeks in a cast, so he and I will work out a schedule where we take turns walking her — Sophie, I mean, not Laura."

Phillip Wilde is my neighbour. He owns Wilde Flowers, the florist next door to Knitorious, and he lives next door to me. We're work neighbours and home neighbours.

Ding! I have a text.

April: Coffee?

Me: Yes! Please!

April and I have been best friends since we met at a Mommy-and-Me group sixteen years ago. Her daughter, Rachel,and my Hannah are the same age and best friends. They're just starting their second semester of university in Toronto. April and her wife, Tamara, also have a son, Zach, who's fifteen, plays hockey, and eats them out of house and home, according to his mothers.

April and Tamara are the owners of Artsy Tartsy, the bakery up the street from Knitorious. Tamara is a talented pastry chef.

About ten minutes after we text, April arrives like a tall, blue-eyed, blonde angel bearing the gift of caffeine. She sets a tray of three to-go cups from the Latte Da café on the counter, then pulls off her mitts, puts them in her coat pockets, and pulls a paper bag from her coat pocket.

"Courtesy of T," she says, dropping the paper bag on the counter. "Dog treats from the latest test batch. We hope Sophie likes them."

I open the bag and remove a small, round, treat that looks like a tennis ball. Sophie is sitting at attention, staring intently at my hand with the treat in it.

She takes her role as taste tester seriously.

"Here you go, Soph!"

I toss the small treat onto her dog bed and she devours it.

"She likes it," I say to April.

Tamara is creating a line of organic, artisanal dog and cat treats to donate to the upcoming silent auction that will benefit our local animal shelter.

Connie and her friends are celebrating their fiftieth high school reunion soon and have decided to host a fundraising event that will be open to the entire town, and will benefit The Vanity Fur Centre for Animal Health & Wellness (us locals call it the Animal Centre or the AC, for short).

Most local businesses are donating items for the silent auction portion of the fundraiser, and April and Tamara are donating pet treats. At least they are if Tamara perfects a recipe she's happy with.

Sophie is part of their focus group and enjoys free samples in exchange for her opinion. Her opinion is always the same: more treats please!

"Have you decided what you're donating to the silent auction yet?" April asks me as she takes a coffee from the tray and hands it to Connie who's sitting on the sofa in the cozy sitting area of the store.

I nod while swallowing my first satisfying sip of coffee and feel its warmth spread through my body. "Yes. The winning bidder will get a bespoke pair of socks, hand knit by me, in a yarn of their choice."

Coffee in hand, I walk over to the cozy sitting area and join them on the comfy, overstuffed furniture.

"I've also been knitting baby blankets using leftover yarn," I say, "for the charity knitting guild's donation to the AC. We have about ten so far. The AC uses them to line the kennels for the shelter animals, and for wrapping up preemie and sick animals to keep them warm."

"Who will be your date, my dear?" Connie asks.

Here we go.

"I'm a confident, independent woman who enjoys her own company and can attend a function alone," I reply.

To be honest, I haven't decided for sure if I'm going yet, but if I do I thought I might take Sophie as my plus one. I could knit her a little corgi-sized dress to wear. It is a fundraiser to benefit animals, after all. And her human, Laura is the founder and executive director of the AC, so it would be appropriate for Sophie to attend. But it might also be weird and earn me a crazy-dog lady label that I don't need.

"You should be dating!" Connie declares, throwing her hands into the air with dramatic flair.

Connie is a hand-talker and gesticulates as a way to visually punctuate when she speaks.

"Thirty-nine is too young to be alone. You should be having fun and meeting people," she says.

"And by people, I mean men," she clarifies, in case I don't know what she means.

April nods in agreement to everything Connie says. It's two against one.

"What do you think Detective Sergeant?" Connie asks, looking behind me. "Don't you agree that Megan is too young for a life of solitude?"

I turn around to see Eric standing near the counter. He's blushing. I look back at Connie who has a look of smug enjoyment on her face for making him blush. She teases him about being shy when he is supposed to be a case-hardened cop.

Eric is my tenant. He lives in the apartment above the store and he's new to Harmony Lake.

Last fall, when Harmony Lake had its first murder ever (technically, our first two murders), the Harmony Lake Police Department borrowed Eric Sloane from a larger department because they didn't have a major crimes unit.

After he solved both murders (with a little help) and prevented a third murder (mine), Harmony Lake implemented a major crimes unit and offered him a job. He is the major crimes unit. Just him.

He's forty-ish, divorced, no kids, and hot. Seriously, he's distractingly attractive. I've had to train myself to not stare.

"Hi Eric," I smile.

I walk over to the counter, silently thanking him for his good timing and interrupting an uncomfortable conversation.

"Hi Megan," He says. "Do you have a package for me?"

I tilt my head and raise my eyebrows. A package? Am I meant to have a package? Did I forget about a package for Eric? I shake my head.

"Phillip was supposed to drop off a package of hand-knit dog sweaters for me to pick up. Laura Pingle is donating them to the silent auction."

I shake my head, "No, Phillip hasn't dropped anything off."

"Amy is expecting me to bring it to the station today."

Officer Amy Andrews is organizing the silent auction portion of the fundraiser. The AC provides free veterinary care for PSD Tundra, Harmony Lake's police dog. Amy is his handler and supporting the AC is important to her. I've heard from some other business owners that she takes her role as organizer seriously. One person likened her to a bride on one of those Bridezilla reality shows.

"I'll text Phillip," I offer.

I text Phillip and ask if he has a package for Eric. While I'm waiting for a response, Connie asks April if there's been any more news about Mega Mart and the AC.

"When I was at the town council meeting in December, the council was divided right down the middle," April says, using her hand like a knife and slicing it through the air. "Laura was there, and she told the pro-Mega-Mart council members that a Mega Mart would go on that land 'over my dead body.' Those were her exact words. Then she said, 'not even over my dead body, because I intend to donate the land before I die to ensure it will always be The Vanity Fur Centre for Animal Health And Wellness.' Then she stomped out of the meeting."

April attends town council meetings on behalf of the Water Street Business Association (WSBA). Each year a different member takes a turn attending the meetings, reporting any relevant details to the rest of the WSBA, and advocating on our behalf.

Ding! I check my phone.

"Laura didn't give him anything for you," I tell Eric, "He says he dropped Laura off at home a couple of hours ago and is going back at lunch to check on her and take her some soup. He says he'll ask her about the sweaters then."

Eric rubs the back of his neck with his hand.

"I'm planning to walk over to Laura's house in a

little while to drop off Sophie. I can ask her for the package and bring it back to the store, if that helps," I offer.

"Why don't I walk over there with you," he suggests, "It'll give me a chance to introduce myself and thank her personally. I'm still the new guy in town, and an introduction from an already-trusted community member like you is always helpful."

He crosses his arms in front of his chest. Don't stare at his chest, Megan.

"Also, I really don't want to show up at the station and see Amy without that package," he adds.

"You two should go now while I'm here to watch the store." Connie makes a sweeping motion with her hands to dismiss us.

"I guess I'll get Sophie and I bundled up," I say, shrugging.

"Great," Eric says, "I'll go get my coat.

ALSO BY REAGAN DAVIS

Killer Cables

Murder & Merino

Twisted Stitches

Son of a Stitch

Crime Skein

Sins & Needles

Rest in Fleece

Life Crafter Death

In Stitchness and in Health

Bait & Stitch

Murder, It Seams

Neigbourhood Swatch: A Knitorious Cozy Mystery Short Story

Sign up for Reagan Davis' email list to be notified of new releases and special offers: https://www.reagandavis.com/email

Follow Reagan Davis on Amazon, Facebook , Instagram, Bookbub, and Goodreads.

ABOUT THE AUTHOR

Reagan Davis is a pen name for the real author who lives in the suburbs of Toronto with her husband, two kids, and a menagerie of pets.

When she's not planning the perfect murder, she enjoys knitting, reading, eating too much chocolate, and drinking too much Diet Coke.

The author is an established knitwear designer who has contributed to several knitting books and magazines. I'd tell you her real name, but then I'd have to kill you. (Just kidding! Sort of.)

http://www.ReaganDavis.com/

ACKNOWLEDGMENTS

This book would not exist without the patience and grace of some very talented people.

Thank you to Kim's Covers for interpreting a vague, and ever-changing vision in my head, and turning it into the perfect cover.

Thank you to Chris and Sherry at The Editing Hall for removing all the double spaces, converting commas that should have been periods, and fixing my sentences when they run like they're being chased (see what I did there!).

Thank you to the beta readers for your honest feedback and patience.

Thank you to the Husbeast and Kidlets for your patience, without you this book would have been published six months sooner.

Made in United States
North Haven, CT
06 September 2023